BONES OF LOVE

Stories of Old Hawaii

By Uldra Johnson

****

*House of Bones

*The Bird Catcher

*Broken Vow

*Warrior Woman

*Where Has He Gone?

*Bones of Love

*Thigh Bone

*The Birthing Stones

For Mary Alice Gamble,

the embodiment of Hawaiian graciousness.

Preface

The respected chronicler of Hawaiian culture, Mary Kawena Pukui, once said that, in Hawaii, unrequited love makes the best stories; hence, most of the old Polynesian legends and myths are tragic in nature. Aptly then, seven of the stories in *Bones of Love* are tragic, though they each express elements of love's sublimity; the title story, "Bones of Love," is the eternal tale, Hawaiian style, of how ultimately, true love triumphs over tragedy.

Na wai e ho'ola i na iwi?
(Who will save the bones?)

HOUSE OF BONES

The old man stooped from under the thatched doorway of the *hale*, emerging from the darkness of the house of bones and gods into the brilliant sunlight, which blinded him for a few moments, so that he closed his eyes and stood stock still, just savoring the warmth that fell on his bony shoulders and hit him in his sunken chest like a golden spear. He always felt groggy and somewhat disoriented after a night with the bones, and this bright morning was no different. He didn't know why this was; perhaps it was because of his ponderous dreams; nevertheless, it was so, and had always been so, for the many years he had been the *kahu* here, the safe-keeper of the kings' bones.

When he reopened his eyes, he gazed with the satisfaction he always knew when he looked upon the environs of this temple, the *heiau* of the ancient king, for, deep in his belly, he felt that this was all his, though of course he never told a soul his thoughts on the matter. Only the highest of high chiefs could enter without his express permission, and even they were courteous and respectful and requested his assistance, rather than making demands. Truly, his life had been good, and for this, he thanked the gods; he would not trade his station in life with the King himself.

His eyes gazed upward to the gentle mountain slopes, where a low-lying rainbow spread its translucent colors across the verdant uplands, which were green with taro,

1

sweet potatoes, sugarcane, bananas and breadfruit. All these good things the people above him brought and gave as offerings. And the people who lived here below, who fished in the calm waters of the bay, on which the heiau stood, brought as offerings the sea's abundance—fish, squid, turtle. Springs and tide pools of fresh waters in this sheltered cove, as well as the many sacred coconut trees, provided him his drink, so that he never thirsted, even during times of drought, when others suffered. As the keeper of the heiau, he too shared in the munificent repast of the bones and gods.

Besides all these material comforts, he was the most protected man in all the islands; there was not man, woman or child living who would dare molest this sacred temple and the keeper of the kings' bones, even during the times of bloodshed, for powerful guardian spirits dwelt here. *Mana*, supernatural power, dwelt in the *iwi*, the bones, and mana dwelt in the wooden images of the gods. Mana was the blessing of the gods and the ancestors, and mana kept evil away. Yes, he was safer than any king, for no king, even his beloved Great King who now slept summer to winter, had enjoyed such security; indeed, he would live to a very old age, and then his own bones would enjoy the honor of resting here with the royal bones and gods. It had been a good life, and he had served well. His bones felt good and satisfied. He closed his eyes and savored again the golden spear of the sun piercing his heart.

Auwe, that feels good to an old man, he thought.

He opened his eyes and stared across the golden sand as his mind drifted to the Great King he had so loved. He felt better now; last night, as he had sat on the beach and watched the eternal stars turn in the black vault of the heavens, he had felt *mehameha*, great loneliness, for the King.

2

The King had been not just his King, but his friend. There had never been, and there would never be again, a King like him! Indeed, was his mana not such, that when the high chiefs had sat in a circle around his lifeless body, which lay upon its deathbed, one had cried, "Let's eat him raw!"

Many times, as young men, he and the Great King had jovially fished together, when times were good and there were no wars. Many a genial repast they had shared together after the war games, when the King, famished by his unrivaled display of almost supernatural strength and agility, would eat food enough for five men, easily consuming a roasted dog, several raw fish, and an entire calabash of *poi*.

In their mid-years, in the prime of their lives, many were the times he had stood reverently near at hand when the King had sacrificed a man to his war god upon the bloodstained stone altar. But the time he liked best to remember was the time of *'ehu ahiahi*, the dust of evening, the time of old age, when the white-haired King would sometimes slip away from his retainers, float through the gathering darkness in his canoe, glide alone through the shadows, and come and sit with him on this very same stone slab on which he now stood.

Then they would talk, two old men, of the glorious past, not just their own past, but the glorious times and deeds of the King's ancestors, whose royal bones lay asleep just inside the doorway. Just as the thatched hale held the bones of the ancient kings, the old man held the cherished memories of the great deeds those bones had done, when they walked in flesh and blood. For this he had lived, and his father before him, and his father before that, a living repository of the royal memories for all his race of people.

He remembered now the last night the King had come, shortly before the fatal sickness. They had talked long and long into the night, while watching the burning stars turn like a heavenly *lei* around the moon. This it was when the King had told him that his royal bones would not rest here, but be hidden where no man could disturb their sleep.

"Only the morning star will know where my bones shall rest," said the King.

The keeper of the bones was greatly surprised, and even greatly offended that the royal bones would be hidden elsewhere.

"There are some who would make fishhooks of my bones," the King had said, and he had laughed softly.

The old kahu had passionately protested this, and assured the King that his bones would be protected with his own life, but the old King had shaken his head sadly, and putting his arm about his old friend, the two had wept together, not so much for the coming of death and separation, as for love.

"*He aikane, he punana na ke onaona*," "A friend is a nest of fragrance," said the King, when the two had finished weeping, and the King rose to go.

"Ku shall remain with you, however," said the King, "and it shall be your duty to safe-keep him."

Those had been his last words, and that had been the last time he had seen his beloved King. Now the old kahu sorely grieved for him.

It was for that reason that he had slept with Ku the Red-feathered, the King's war god, last night. No other man living, not even the King's own son, would dare lie down with Ku. He chuckled to think of it, of how he had removed the god on the stick from the *tapa* bundle and lain down on the stone floor of the heiau as if he were sleeping with a beloved wife. In the moonlight that had filtered through the thatched roof, he had become heavy-eyed while staring into the distended mouth, large rows of sharks' teeth and pearl-shelled eyes, and he had gone to the

4

land of dreams with the red feathers of Ku the war god tickling his chin, as he held him close in a love embrace.

The old man's slow gaze now took in the wooden *ki'i* that stood upon the low pedestals in the sand and the high posts on the rocks that jutted over the edge of the sea, the carved wooden gods who warned away intruders with their fierce grimaces and frightful forms. Yes, he felt better now, for last night the gods and old kings had spoken to him in his dreams, and directed him to a sacred task. Today he would begin; he would reclothe with precious *tapa* cloth and flower lei the ki'i that protected the temple, the wooden gods that now stood naked, their former garments now tattered shreds, sadly decayed and bleached by the sun.

How he would obtain the tapa cloth and flower lei he did not yet know. The people, he knew, were afraid to make the traditional offerings to the temple, for the new King, the Great King's son, and his foster mother, had forbidden the worship of the old gods. They still brought the food offerings, however, but these they handed directly to the kahu, so that they would not be guilty of transgressing the new law. The new King, nothing like the old King, who had revered the gods and the ancestors, had in fact razed every heiau in the land, except this one. This temple alone stood, the most sacred in all the islands, for in it rested the bones of the greatest kings who had ever lived. Even the new King would not dare lift a finger against the bones of his own forefathers.

The old man sighed now when he thought of the changes that had happened since the Great King's death. He himself had been a young man when the white strangers had sailed in. He and the King, who was not king then but a young chief, had stood on the beach together and marveled at the floating islands, the ships with the sails as high as coconut trees. The commoners and the chiefs and even his own father, the high priest, had thought the strangers gods; it was the women who first reported that these strangers groaned in love, and when the people, the chiefs and the priests saw with their own eyes how the strangers also groaned in death, they knew they were not gods, but men like themselves.

The white strangers had departed, and for many years were not seen again, though they were never forgotten, and talked of much, but one day they had returned, and since that dark day, everything had changed. The Great King, as long as he lived, had protected his people and his gods with his superior cunning against these saucy strangers who had greater weapons, greater ships, and destructive waters that made a man wild and feeble-minded when he drank them. But when the Great King died, and the faltering son, who, at the sly urging of the strangers, imbibed the bad waters, and then cried like a baby, became ruler of the islands, the strangers with their bad ways had turned the kingdom from good to evil.

Of the new King it had been whispered that he was "*pupule ka moa, 'a'ohe puka mimi*," "a chicken that is crazy, it has no urine vent." To the great shock of commoners and chiefs alike, one evening very soon after the Great King his father had died, he had sat down, and against the ancient will of the gods, had eaten with women, and then with a drunken sweep of his hand, had decreed that the old gods, the temples, and the *kapus*, the divine laws, were to be destroyed forever.

The old man shook his head again, and stepped off the stone slab, muttering as he crossed the sandy temple grounds, where profusions of waxy green *pohuehue*, beach morning glory vines, were just opening their lavender blossoms toward the sun, and among which bees hummed happily. He passed the awful-visaged *ki'i akua*, the protector god that stood twelve feet tall. With his head many times larger than his body, his huge tongue protruding from his gaping mouth, and his erect phallus, symbol of mana, divine power, he warned would-be trespassers of no entry. Several sheets of bleached tapa, in tattered shreds, hung from the god's neck.

I shall reclothe him today, the old man determined to himself, and he mentally sent a prayer to the gods for their help in the matter.

Children were playing outside the palisade made of palm trunks that surrounded the sacred precincts of the heiau, and he stopped to watch, as he did each morning, for a child's laughter meant much to him, now that he was an old man. The smallest child, a bashful, raven-haired, sweet-eyed girl, ran to him and placed a pohuehue blossom in his hand, and then shyly ran away again. An enormous black stone, the Stone-For-Looking-At-The-Sun, which not one hundred men could move, rested on the edge of a pool of water, projecting over and into it so that it formed an underwater tunnel. He watched as a small child dove into the water and through the tunnel, and then emerged wide-eyed and laughing joyously.

"Did you see the bright glowing green ball?" asked the old kahu, bending over and smiling down at the child, "Did you see the sparkling pearl?" —for if the brilliant light of the ball of the sun were just right, so that the refraction of the water and the shadow of the stone mixed together, such magical things might be seen by a wide-eyed child. The old man knew, for as a child, he had himself seen these things many times in this very pool.

The child laughed without answering, and scrambling from the pool raced to join the other splashing and frolicking children. The old man watched as the next child dove into the tunnel, while the others gamboled and pranced about the edge of the pool like little puppies.

"Watch your *iwi puniu*," he called to the children. "Take heed of your coconut shells."

By this, he warned them to watch out for their heads. But just as he had done as a child, the children paid the warning no mind. The next child ran at full speed and plunged recklessly headfirst beneath the stone, followed by another who skipped to the edge singing a lilting song to *mo'o*, the lizard spirit god who protected the pool; the child then gracefully dove beneath the surface. The old man stood and stared fixedly into the water ripples with the deadly concentration of a fisher bird; in a moment, a string of glistening bubbles floated from the puffed cheeks of a small brown face emerging from the water tunnel. He could tell when the children saw the magic, for their eyes would grow big and their faces would become distorted with wonder, so that they looked like strange, big-eyed, intoxicated fish. The old man laughed, for the happy children brought back good memories.

Children know, he thought.

He waved his hand to the children, but they were playing too absorbedly to wave back. He chuckled and turned toward the path down to the water's edge, walking with shuffling steps, looking at the ground, as old men do. He could still hear the children's laughter, and he was thinking what a pleasant morning it was, and wondering how many more he would have. When he looked up again and looked out to sea, what he saw made his heart stop, and he dropped the lavender flower he held in his hand.

Rounding the curve of the bay came a number of canoes, and he saw immediately by the hats and bright colors of the clothing that they contained white men, *haoles*. He no longer heard the children's laughter, and the pleasantry of the bright morning instantly faded away.

What are they doing here? he thought. What do they want?

Sure enough, about a dozen white men, rowed by stalwart natives, were heading directly for the heiau. With them were two high chiefs of the island, with several retainers. The white men were talking and laughing among themselves while the natives paddled in silence.

One of the high chiefs, the Governor of the island, a colossal man wearing a native *malo* around his loins, and a white man's dress jacket much too tight for his fleshy frame, but of which he was immensely proud, was smiling and gesturing in an exaggerated manner, but the other chief, who ruled this district of the island and was guardian of the lands of the heiau, sat grim-faced and stared straight ahead.

One of the white men, evidently an artist, was making a quick sketch of the bay while talking to the Captain.

"This is the last of the pagan temples," the Captain was saying. "I wouldn't say that this is an honor, but it is a bit of a treat. No white man has ever been allowed to enter the threshold; for that matter, neither has a commoner ever entered, for it contains the most precious relics of the people, the bones of the kings. A sort of mausoleum, if you please. Yes, I believe you could call it a mausoleum. Probably won't be here much longer. I understand it's a bit of an embarrassment to the Queen Regent, who was instrumental in influencing the late King her foster son to rid the land of the ancient idols and do away with the taboos. I understand she wants the place disassembled. The Queen Regent has become a staunch Christian, thanks to the missionaries. She is desperate to be baptized in the Church."

"We'll disassemble it all right," interjected a boisterous, haole sailor, a wiry-looking, sun-creased fellow with a bulbous red nose. He drew a flask from out his pocket and took a hearty nip.

"Speaking of mausoleums," said the artist, ignoring the sailor, as he continued to sketch, "I understand that the late King…"

"Bless his burning behind!" hooted the boisterous sailor, and he turned around and made a crude gesture with his backside.

9

"Why do you say that?" asked the artist, looking up at the boisterous sailor, who took another nip from the flask, and then wiped his mouth with the back of a dirty hand.

"Because it was death to be behind his backside," yelled the sailor, snickering loudly. "Very hot back there." The man laughed insanely, so that the native paddlers stared at him.

"Strange taboos these people had," explained the Captain to the artist, who was a young Englishman of the genteel class. "The late King could not be approached from behind, nor could anyone touch his back, or it was instant death. There was one queen whose shadow was not to fall on anyone, including herself. She had to go about at night to prevent killing a poor soul. And as you know, men and women were not allowed to eat together, upon pain of death. Much of the food was taboo for women—coconuts, bananas…"

"Not anymore, praise Lucifer!" yelled the boisterous sailor. "Those sweet little brown wahines know who to come to now when they want a good banana!"

The artist gave the crude fellow little notice but addressed the Captain again.

"As I was saying, I understand that the late King absolutely refused to go into Westminster Abbey."

"That's right," answered the Captain. "He was game for everything else in London—dressed like an English gent, went to the Opera House, the Theatre, the fancy-dress balls—but at Westminster he would only stand before the door and look foolish. Nothing could persuade him to enter. He said the bones of the English kings were sacred and he wasn't blood connected. He felt he had no right to walk around their caskets. He said to even step foot there would be to desecrate the place. The place was taboo, he said."

10

"Humble chap," yelled the boisterous sailor. "Right might he well be too. Not too right in the 'ead. Not a bit like his father the old King. Now there was a bloke!"

The artist looked at the Captain questioningly. The Captain glanced at the nearby canoe carrying the Governor, who most certainly could hear this conversation, though how much he could understand the Captain could only guess. The Governor waved and smiled back broadly, for he had his own reasons for befriending the sailors—he had a number of native goods he intended to sell to the haoles at a high profit.

"It's true," said the Captain. "The late King was rather weak, couldn't measure up in any fashion or form to the Great King his father. Seems that the white man's liquor went to his head early in life. The Great King knew his son was not fit to be king, and that's why he appointed his favorite wife as Queen Regent to govern with his heir. Maybe he saw, or maybe he didn't, how she would take total control of the islands. At any rate, the son didn't care; he was content to eat, drink and sport about with his wives and his royal yacht. It's said that at his entertainments he would command that salutes be fired from the fort each time his royal lips took a sip. He traded the entire islands' sandal wood forests, and the backs of the people, for that ship, and scuttled it soon after he got it, while drunk. I think he realized he couldn't govern, and that is why he wanted to visit King George in England."

"Needed a bit of fatherly advice," interjected the lively sailor, whose eyes were beginning to look bloodshot.

"He wanted to place the islands under our protection," said the Captain. "Too bad he never got to see King George."

"Yes," said the artist, "a bit sad how he died. Just a case of the measles. And his queen too. Was she really a giantess?"

11

"She was," said the Captain. "A six-foot seven-inch chiefess. Quite a beauty too, I understand."

"Must be an exception," replied the artist, with a disparaging smile, "for I have never in all my life seen such disgusting looking creatures as these royal chiefesses —most hideous faces and misshapen corpulent bodies, not a tolerably good-looking woman among them."

The Captain glanced toward the Governor, who, however, was occupied in eating a raw fish. He lowered his voice.

"Perhaps so; he had five wives and this one was his favorite," said the Captain. "His half-sister too. In fact, all of his wives were sisters or nieces."

The boisterous sailor made a face. "I 'eared," he shouted, "that's why he wouldn't 'ear of becoming Christian; didn't want to give up 'is five wives."

"Is it true he died for love, is it true he just took sick and died when his queen died?" asked the artist.

"Seems so," answered the Captain. "He was stricken first but was on the mend. Then she took it and died. King George sent his best doctors over to their hotel, but the royal chap just seems to have given up."

"A sort of tragedy, I suppose," said the artist, looking at his sketch critically, "is it true about her dying in his arms?"

"Yes," said the Captain. "When they saw she was going, they brought him to her bedside and lifted him into her bed; he was very weak, you know. Then they left them alone together. It's said that the royal attendants were shocked because the King never in his life had been left alone without an attendant, and at first, they refused to go. The King himself had to order them, though he could hardly whisper. When they returned after an hour, she had died. Story goes that the King held her in a tight embrace and refused to let go for two days; they had to pry his fingers from her lifeless body. A bit romantic, I suppose."

"A sort of pity," replied the artist. "I understand the people here were very taken with her."

"Yes, she was a great favorite," said the Captain. "Seems she had a sort of presentiment of death. It's said that thousands wept and wailed when she embarked on the ship for England. I heard that she stopped on the gangway and sang to the people."

"Sang to the people?" asked the artist.

"It's a quaint custom they have," explained the Captain. "On every emotional occasion, which is quite often—for remember, we are dealing here with a very childlike people, given to colorful display— at any rate, they spontaneously create chants. Seems a sort of talent they have."

At this, the boisterous sailor called over to the Governor. "Say, my man, can you sing what the late Queen sang to the people when she left for old England?"

The corpulent chief wiped his bloody fingers on his jacket, proudly drew his enormous chest up, smiled fawningly at the white men in the nearby canoe, and began chanting in a strong, rich voice, in the melodious language of his own people, words that meant: "O heavens, O plains, O mountains and oceans, O guardians and people, love to you all! Farewell to thee, country, the land, O country for which my father toiled. Farewell to thee!"

When he had finished chanting, he made a grand flourish with his arms spread wide toward the white men's canoe. Immediately the sailor jumped to his feet, rocking the canoe, so that he almost fell overboard. He spread his arms wide in imitation of the Governor, and in a high singsong voice, bawled out a string of unintelligible syllables that meant nothing to either the natives or the haoles. Then he took off his cap and threw it at the Governor, yelling, "That's for you, matey."

The white men in the canoes laughed, but the Governor looked sheepish as the cap fell to his feet in the

13

canoe. The other high chief still sat hard-faced and silent, looking straight ahead.

"If he was such a bad king," asked the artist, "how is it there was such an uproar among the populace when we returned with his and the Queen's remains? You would have thought it was King George himself! There were thousands of natives, hugging, weeping, rubbing noses!"

"It's the way of these people," explained the Captain. "An overly-emotional, easily excited race, when it comes to their chiefs, no matter how badly they rule or how ineptly. Loyal chaps the commoners are."

"So did they actually perform human sacrifices in this temple?" asked the artist, changing the subject.

"They did," said the Captain. "According to what I have been told, for every post and rafter erected, a human sacrifice was made. It's estimated that at least eighty sacrifices were offered just in the construction of this heiau. And every time a chief was deposited here, at every stage of the so-called consecration of the bones, a sacrifice was made.

"They would wrap the body in banana and taro leaves, bury it in a shallow grave, and burn it for some days, the same way they roast pigs. Then they scraped the flesh from the bones and arranged them by placing those of the left side of the body together and those of the right side together. The long bones of the arms and legs were stained scarlet red, which signified royalty. They tied the bundle of bones together with human hair, with the skull on top, wrapped it in black tapa cloth and then sometimes encased this in a sort of woven casket.

"They would take the flesh that had been scraped from the bones, wrap it in black tapa, and on a certain night declare a taboo so that every light in the land had to be extinguished and no sound could be made, even the cry of a baby, on pain of death, while they buried the flesh at sea. At each step of the process, a man was sacrificed."

14

The artist made a wry face, and the Captain continued.

"Of course, there were other sacrifices too. War prisoners, taboo-breakers, sacrifices to propitiate the gods. I heard a tale of just a few years ago about a queen, still living, who sent her servant, a small child, her personal favorite, to filch a banana for her from the men's eating-house. Of course, bananas being taboo for women, it was a crime meriting death. When it was discovered, the kahuna, the witch doctor, ordered that the boy die in place of the queen. He was strangled on the altar by the high priest."

"Ghastly heathenish," replied the artist. "When did they stop these ungodly sacrifices?"

"Not so long ago," said the Captain. "The last one took place here during the time of the Great King, about six years ago, a year before the Great King expired. One poor chap was sacrificed for wearing the malo, the loincloth, of a chief. Another was offered to their gods for eating taboo food. The last was a woman put to death for entering the eating-house of her husband when she was drunk."

"Yet such a peaceful and beautiful cove," said the artist, nodding toward the beach. "Who could guess that such appalling happenings once took place here."

"At one time," said the Captain, "I understand that this whole cove sheltered a large village, the ancestral home of the Great King. It was called *pu'uhonua*, which meant it was a place of refuge; refugees of various kinds—criminals and pursued warriors, taboo breaker—could receive absolution if they could get here alive. But the water is too shallow for our ships, so the Great King decided to move his main residence to better harbors, for he was keen on commerce. Then later, when the son of the Great King broke the kapu system, there was no longer any need to come here for absolution, for the religion had

15

been annulled, so the place went into decline. When the missionaries arrived, the people were introduced to our God of Mercy. But in Cook's time, this was a place of importance. The most sacred heiau in the islands."

"Did Cook himself come here?" asked the artist.

"Some of his officers visited, but of course they weren't allowed to enter the heiau. Only other whites to come here were some missionary chaps, but they were strictly forbidden also. Quite a treat it is to be the first white men to step foot in one of these horrifying temples. Quite good of the Queen Regent to give us permission to do what we want."

One of the other white men pointed toward the fence that enclosed the temple. On a stone wall stood a number of curiously carved wooden poles.

"What are those odd things?" he asked.

"Those are, I believe, the ki'i, the gods' protectors," said the Captain.

By this time the canoes had pulled up to shore, and the native paddlers jumped out and began securing them on the beach. The Captain, the artist, and the white officers and sailors quickly disembarked, and, without waiting for the corpulent Governor, who was being helped out of his precariously-rocking canoe by his retainers, began walking briskly toward the heiau.

Their eyes looked straight ahead at the object of their interest as they talked eagerly among themselves, and they strode right past, without seeing, the old kahu who stood on the path in an attitude of great dignity, waiting to welcome them. The quiet chief, who followed behind the haoles, made a sign of respect to the kahu, but the corpulent Governor, who labored to catch up to the group, failed to acknowledge the kahu in his hurry.

The haole Captain and sailors strode past the pool and the Stone-For-Looking-at-the-Sun, behind which the children shrank back, their large brown eyes both curious and shy.

Before the entrance of the palisade stood the twelve-foot-high wooden guardian, the ki'i akua, the idol with his head many times larger than his body, with his huge tongue protruding from huge mouth, and his phallus erect, warning them against trespassing. But the Captain and his sailors, after a single distasteful glance, strode purposefully right through the palisade, and only were stopped from proceeding further by the eerie courtyard scene that met their eyes.

Startling male and female wooden images, ten feet high, stood on low pedestals and high posts at unequal distances all around; all of the male idols stood with knees bent, and phalluses erect, as if ready to spring upon some ill-fated victim and tear him apart. A semicircle of twelve frightful deities stood on pillars on a pile of stones in the form of a crescent. In the center of these stood a strange, finely-carved deity, with a child in its arms, and an equally strange black figure of a man, resting on his fingers and toes, with his head inclined backwards. Before each image were decayed offerings—large piles of broken calabashes, old coconut shells, rotten wreaths of flowers and branches and fragments of tapa cloth. A wooden scaffold, made of poles more than fourteen feet high, stood on one side of the courtyard.

This, the breathless Governor explained, as he came up behind the men, was the 'anu'u, the oracle tower. Poles with curiously carved wooden heads stood about the courtyard and on the stone walls—some grimacing, some frowning, some with evil smiles or gaping mouths that threatened to eat one alive.

"Great unholy guns!" exclaimed the boisterous sailor, and he pulled out his flask and took a long swig, while his blood-shot eyes took in the scene before him.

"Good God!" said the artist. "What uncouth forms!"

17

"Frightfully obscene!" said the Captain.

"It's enough to turn a man's stomach," said one sailor. And then he added, "I'm gonna get me one of these."

The group of white men recovered from their initial awe and strode as a group quickly toward the thatched hale, the house of the bones. They had paused just long enough to enable the old kahu to hobble across the courtyard and reach the thatched doorway of the sacred house. In his agitation and hurry to stop the men, he stumbled over the door stone, and nearly fell, but recovered his balance and tottering, turned and stood with his back against the doorway, holding his bony arms outspread, with his palms pressed against the wall of the hale.

"Kapu, kapu!" he cried out in alarm.

"Who's that?" asked the artist, drolly.

"This must be the priest," said the Captain, and the Governor nodded.

"You want me to dispatch 'em, Cap'in?" said the boisterous sailor, who now had a mean and hungry look in his bloodshot eyes.

"Not yet," said the Captain, "let our good Governor try some logic."

The Captain waited patiently for the Governor, who walked smilingly to where the Captain stood before the old kahu. The Governor began to speak to the old man in his own language, all the while beaming broadly, in a mixture of condescension and flattery. The old man, however, whose face first drained of blood, and then became contorted with anger, began talking and gesturing frantically, pointing at the heiau and then at the white men.

"What's he saying?" asked the artist.

"I think our good Governor is explaining to the old chap that we intend to make a visit," said the Captain, who crossed his arms now with impatience, for he expected to be back at his ship for the dinner hour.

And that was what the Governor was explaining. The Governor was telling the old kahu the news that the King, the son of the Great King, had died in England, and his wife too, and that these most honorable white men had kindly brought the bones of the King and his Queen all the way home from across the wide seas. The Queen Regent had extended therefore every hospitality to these white men, in appreciation, with her people's gratitude. When the Governor explained further that authority had been given to allow the white men to enter the heiau and take whatever they wanted, the old man's face became white with indignation and rage. He looked toward the grim-faced chief, who averted his eyes.

At this point the Captain, who had only so much patience, and who was curious to see the interior of the sacred house, and who wanted to be back to his ship for the dinner hour, brushed by the old man on the stone step, and the artist and soldiers followed.

"Better move yerself, old man, before yer get 'urt," said the boisterous sailor, and he seized the old man by the elbows, lifted him up roughly and set him down the step.

After ducking through the low doorway, the Captain and his men stood for a moment while their eyes adjusted to the darkness, for the only illumination was from the small entrance. What they beheld was far stranger than what they had seen in the courtyard.

Two large, elaborately carved idols with inhuman visages, over five feet tall, which the Governor soon explained were *akua mo'i*, lords of the god, stood behind the stone altar, facing them. Near the right side of the door were bundles of deified bones, beginning with the most ancient of the kings. These were wrapped in caskets woven of coconut fiber, and resembled the human form; especially the outline of the skull was obviously human. They were adorned with feathered helmets and hideous masks ornamented with rows of sharks' teeth and tufts of human hair.

"E gads," exclaimed the boisterous sailor, "a bloody charnel house!"

The corpulent Governor, with some difficulty, entered through the doorway, followed by the grim-faced chief, and the old kahu. The grim-faced chief walked solemnly to a bundle of bones, removed his tapa shoulder covering and placed it with great care over a bundle of bones. The Captain saw him, and inquired of the Governor the reason.

"He has kinsman here," explained the Governor, and the Governor smiled broadly.

The artist, having a keen eye for detail, was the first to remark how, in spite of the differences, the masks all preserved a strong likeness to one another. The Governor smilingly explained that indeed this was true, for all these were ancient kings of the same lineage.

Heaped up like so much firewood in one corner were naked bones—mostly leg bones, arm bones, and skulls, some of them not yet dry. These, the Governor explained, were the bones of great warriors. On the left were large tapa bundles on which feathers or wooden idols rested.

In two corners were stacked calabashes and shells containing fishhooks and various items, including a wood-carved toy canoe; while against the walls were sixteen-foot-long spears, drums, and, curiously, a Chinese mask. The floor was strewn with debris from various offerings and remains of tapa. Weapons of various kinds, among them daggers, slings and strangling cords, as well as rotting feather garments, were placed without any seeming order among the relics.

The Captain and his men walked among the various effigies, articles, and bones at first in silence, while the artist hastily began to sketch, for he knew he had only moments.

"Call to your men," the Captain said peremptorily to the Governor. "I should like the two odd figures there by the altar."

The Captain walked about choosing other items he wanted—a couple of spears, some calabashes, several of the effigies, and one of the drums. He also took all of the masks and the toy canoe. The Governor called his retainers, who in turn called down to the natives who lingered outside the courtyard. The men were commanded to load into the canoes the articles the Captain had chosen. When the Captain had everything he wanted, he stooped beneath the door and went once again into the courtyard, where he supervised the natives who carried the spoils down to the canoes.

The artist meanwhile was furiously sketching the interior of the sacred house. Now that the Captain had taken any thing he might want, the sailors began appropriating what they wanted. The spears and remaining weapons were snatched up immediately. The Governor, glancing sideways at the kahu, and then at the grim-faced chief, slipped the Chinese mask under his arm. When the artist saw what was happening, he threw down his sketchpad and rushed for two beautiful spears, and then for the feathered deity that covered the bones of the most ancient of the Kings. At this, the old kahu cried out and charged toward the artist, but he was held back by a hand on his shoulder and a look of warning from the Governor.

Within ten minutes, the sacred house had been ransacked. In the commotion, a number of items had been broken; bits of calabashes and bits of helmets, tattered red and gold feathers from the wooden gods, littered the floor. All that was left was the stone altar, which would have been taken, if it had been more portable, and the bones themselves, which also would have been taken, but that the old kahu threw himself upon them, and, as the sailors later said, "showed some signs of regret," so that they left the bones to him.

"Who wants some bloody old bones anyway?" they quipped, laughing and gesturing toward the old man who lay prostrate across the wickerwork casket of the most ancient king, clutching it tightly. They stooped under the doorway, carrying their newly acquired spears and calabashes and idols, and the old kahu was left alone in the dark of the house.

He lay in the dark for some minutes, his heaving bony frame covering the wickerwork casket of bones, shaking from his head to his feet. A painful spasm in his chest and a large lump in his throat made him think that perhaps he was now dying. From the courtyard, he could hear loud voices—commanding voices, laughing voices, derisive voices. He felt too exhausted, too weak to rise, but when the voices ceased, and all was quiet, he forced himself to his feet. He looked about the sacred house, for now he remembered that the most important thing was Ku. Had not the Great King commanded him to protect Ku, his war god? With horror, he realized that Ku was gone. Trembling all over, he staggered to the doorway and stooped under, emerging into brilliant sunlight.

The courtyard where the wooden gods had presided was now empty; not a god remained. Only the stumps of some of the ki'i were left from where they had been forcibly hacked from their pilings in the sand. Not one of the carved gods that had stood sentinel on the stone wall still stood. The decayed offerings of coconuts, flowers, and pieces of tapa had been trampled about by the heavy boots of the sailors, so that bits of rubbish were everywhere. Tracks in the sand showed where the largest wooden gods had been hauled by ropes toward the beach and the canoes. The pohuehue vines with their lavender flowers were broken and crushed. The 'anu'u, the oracle tower, alone remained, stark and forbidding.

22

From the beach came the sound of the sailors loading their spoils. The old kahu walked unsteadily as fast as he could, for his knees wobbled and he panted for breath. When he passed through the palisade, he saw with horror that the wooden guardian figure, the fierce ki'i akua, with his head many times larger than his body, with the huge tongue protruding from his mouth, was gone—he had been crudely plucked by his root so that only a broken stub of splintered wood remained.

The kahu hurried as fast as his spindly legs would go, down the trail to the beach. He passed the Stone-For-Looking-At-The-Sun, where the little children stood, solemn and thoughtful, as if they had been rebuked for some wrongdoing that they did not understand. They looked at the old man sympathetically with big brown eyes, and the smallest child timidly waved a hand to the old man, but the old kahu, blinded by the strong sunlight and his agitation, didn't see. His heart beat wildly, his vision was strangely blurred, and he stumbled over a small ki'i. The wooden god lay broken on the path, apparently abandoned as worthless by the haoles and tossed aside.

Suddenly three tipsy sailors, one of them the boisterous nipper, who had been generously sharing his flask, strode up the path toward the old kahu; for in fact, they had been sent by the Captain to seek him out. The Captain, who had been "touched" as he had said, by the old man's "rectitude and loyalty, pagan though he be," had sent the sailors to console him by some presents of a knife, some beads, an old suit of clothes, and an old sailor's cap.

They surrounded the old man, joking and laughing, so that the old man didn't know what they were up to. When one of the men held up the knife, the old man frantically shielded his face with his thin arms. This caused the sailors to laugh uproariously, and one of them hooted loudly and slapped the old man on the back, so that he lost his balance and lurched forward.

"Aye, I don't believe he likes this 'ere knife," said one soldier, and the other grabbed it from him and said, "Give it me. I know a pretty brown wench it will buy."

Another sailor caught the confused kahu and quickly stuffed the old clothes in his trembling hands, while the third sailor, by now quite under the influence, squashed the sailor's cap on the old man's head.

The first sailor now noticed the children standing by The-Stone-For-Looking-at-the- Sun, and he called to them, "Here kiddy, kiddy, kiddy," but the children, all except the smallest child, shrank back behind the great stone, and hid their faces. The sailor quickly advanced a few steps and placed the beads over the head of the one small girl who had not run away, who now stood clutching her elbows, looking up at him seriously and silently. The three jovial sailors then turned and strode back toward the beach, jocularly pushing and shoving one another as they went, while they passed the flask between them.

The old kahu stood as if struck by lightening; then in fury, he tossed the old suit of clothes to the ground. He removed the cap from his head, looked at for a moment, and then flung it into the dust at his feet. He stumbled on as fast as his old legs could carry him, like an old long-legged spider on the run.

The last of the spoils were being loaded into the canoes when the old kahu reached the beach. The sailors, in a burst of merriment, had placed the idol holding the child in the stern of a canoe, so that it looked like a ludicrous figurehead. The beautifully carved black figure of the man resting on his fingers and toes was dumped unceremoniously upside down amid a heap of calabashes, swords, and masks in the Captain's canoe.

Some sort of squabble seemed to be happening with the Governor, for he had taken this as an auspicious time to present a number of island curiosities for sale, at an exorbitant price, to the haoles. He was on board the Captain's canoe, holding a scarlet and gold feather capelet.

"Hand the pudding head over!" shouted a sailor.

"I'll hand our fat friend over!" shouted another, and the two of them hustled the Governor rudely overboard, where, with a mortified expression on his face, his corpulent self was hauled into a rocking canoe by his retainers.

"How dare the mercenary rogue!" complained the Captain to his men, as they pushed off from shore, for, though the Captain was usually reserved in his emotions, and known to be generous with the natives, he was at present indignant. "To think that we should pay for what we can receive gratis from the hands of these people!"

The old kahu waded into the water, and tried to shout to the sailors, "*Kali iki, kali iki*!" —"Wait, wait a moment!" but the thickness in his throat caused his voice to sound strange and small and the canoes sailed on; not one sailor looked back. The Governor and his men had also pushed off from shore, and the old man was left alone, under the hot mid-morning sun. He stood in the shallows, watching them go; a red feather drifted about his feet.

For a long time the old man stood, looking with dim eyes off into the distance, where the silver waves undulated like magic in the white light of the morning. Porpoises were splashing and playing about the canoes, as they disappeared around the palm-studded cove. At last, the old man turned and walked up the path to the heiau, and never did an old man walk more slowly, falteringly, and dejectedly.

As he neared The-Stone-For-Looking-At-The-Sun, he saw the children, standing all-in-a-row, solemn-eyed and silent. He stopped and placed his quaking hands on the stone, supporting himself for a few moments, resting. The children stood and stared.

After a time, he gathered his strength and wandered slowly on, staring down at the sand. The children, silent and somber, stepped onto the sandy path, and soundlessly followed the sad old man at a distance. When he reached the entrance to the palisade, he stopped, and looked up. The children came forward quietly and gathered in a semi-circle around him, watching his face.

There, placed with small loving hands, on the broken stump of wood where once the fearful ki'i akua, the great guardian of the temple had stood with his head many times larger than his body and his huge tongue protruding from his mouth—supported by branches, was the broken ki'i that had been abandoned as worthless by the haoles. An old shirt and a tattered coat were draped over two pieces of driftwood that were stuck in the sand before the image, for a body of sorts; shiny glass beads adorned the ragged shirt, and a frayed sailor's cap was jammed onto the god's head. A few red feathers and a strand of waxy green pohuehue vine lay at the god's feet; a single lavender pohuehue flower had been placed on the god's erect phallus.

The expectant, kindly faces of the little children, with their bright, brown eyes, stood looking up at the old man, wondering if he would like it.

THE BIRD CATCHER

With the long and shiny black wing feathers of the *'alala* sticking out from his shaggy head, scruffy grey bristles sticking out on his chin, and dirty yellowish-brown fluff poking out from his ears, so that he looked like a walking untidy bird's nest, the bird catcher hid in the trees directly above the cliff and watched the beach of the cove directly below. Sooner or later, she would appear, he knew. If he were lucky, she would emerge from her hut naked, because it was her way to wander about without clothing, since no one ever came here; that is, that she knew of. The bird catcher giggled to himself. Or, if not that, he thought, and he scratched his groin, she might remove her kapa when she bathed in the sea. He had only to wait long enough, he knew.

The king's bird catcher was very good at waiting. In fact, no one could match the bird catcher at waiting. He could sit patiently for hours and hours, every now and then whistling the song of the bird he wanted to seize, for he knew all the songs of the different birds, and in this way, he lured them to his gummy pole.

They would fly happily down to alight on the flowers attached to the crosspiece of the pole, and then they would stick fast in the juice of the *papala kepau* tree. He had other tricky means of taking them too, for he was very wily, the bird catcher. He had nooses that he hid on the ground for the ground birds, geese and such, and he had snares that he concealed in the branches of the trees, with which he caught big birds such as owls and hawks. He also had netting with which he could entangle birds of all sizes, and he had little nets on sticks with which he would climb trees at night and snatch all the surprised, night-blind occupants of a nest, mother and father and baby birds. If he should find little eggs, and if he were very hungry, he ate them then and there, while sitting in the tree. One, two—he plopped the little delicacies in his mouth and savored them, then spat out the shells violently through the black gaps between his teeth.

Every few months, when he passed this wooded way, in his search for sacred feathers used to make the costly-feathered cloaks and feather *kahili* standards for the king, he would make a long detour to this place where she dwelled in isolation, just to spy on her. Though she was growing older, she was still comely.

When she had first come here, to live alone—because she had the mark of the gods on her—she had been friendly, and sometimes when she encountered him on the forest paths, she had smiled, looking down on him, for she was straight and tall like the sugar cane, while he was short and stocky. They would talk, for this was a lonely place, even for such a one as she, and this was the land of the terrible volcano goddess; few wandered here. She would be eager for news, for in his wanderings about the country, he knew everyone and all that was happening round about the land, whereas she rarely left her secluded dwelling place.

Sometimes she would sit for a while and he would teach her to whistle the melodic songs and the mating calls of the various forest birds. She would purse her lips prettily, and mimic him so easily, that he was quite surprised. He had taught her the prayer chant to the Bird God, and he had revealed to her many secrets of the winged creatures. He would risk giving her some precious scarlet feathers of the little *i'iwe* bird, or a prized golden

28

feather of the *mamo* bird, which treasures were kapu to all but the king, and for which risk he would lose his life, if it were known; in this way, he hoped to win her affection and then her favors.

She never asked him his name, but always called him "Bird Catcher," which somewhat annoyed him. One time, hoping for a bit more intimacy, he began to boast.

"My name is Halulu," he said, and he thrust his hairy chest out like a cunning old crow. "Perhaps you have heard of me before coming here?"

She smiled, and confessed that she had not.

"The king himself gave me my name," he said, and he cast his eyes down with sham modesty. "I am named for the *halulu* bird, the bird that can take on any human form he wishes."

As she just smiled to this, and said nothing, so that he took her smile for admiration, he continued, "I am Halulu, named for the mighty bird whose feathers are made of water particles from the dazzling orb of the sun, whose every feather is tipped by a tearing talon."

To demonstrate Halulu's legendary prowess, he spread his short hairy arms out like wings, puffed his furry chest out even further, and turned slowly round in a circle, but when he stopped, she was already picking up her calabash from the ground, and had not even noticed his display of playfulness, so that he felt hot and foolish.

Just the same, whenever she encountered him, she called him, "Bird Catcher."

One time he had offered to show her his crude hut, where he sometimes slept when he was in this area, and where he made offerings to the god of bird catchers, Ku-huluhulu-manu. She followed him trustingly, for she wished to see the altar to the bird-god. But once there, because her smile was friendly and her way so engaging, he had suddenly grabbed her and pressed her to him, and she had responded by repulsing him with obvious revulsion.

She had snarled at him with such abhorrence and her eyes had blazed with such fierce intention that he had stumbled backward, and then she angrily had reminded him that she was a *kilo*, a reader of omens, a stargazer, and had devoted herself to the sacred gods. He had taken her angry look and her words as a warning and a threat, and had let her go, for who knew what powers she possessed? After all, she was of the Pele clan, and the goddess of fire was the most feared deity of all the gods. Truly, perhaps she herself was that dreadful goddess, for it was well known Pele took many forms, and why else would a young woman live fearlessly in this lonely place? Thereafter, if they met on the forest paths, she spurned him with obvious distaste, so that he felt dirty and loathsome. Still, he both longed for her and hated her.

He rubbed the black bristle on his chin, scratched his crotch, and waited.

Soon she did appear, to his disappointment, wearing an old kapa. He watched while she worked at various things, but when she picked up a calabash and started down the beach, he knew she would be gathering seaweed all morning, and soon out of close sight. This was the only vantage point from which to spy on her, for the cove was bounded in both directions by sheer cliff walls, and there was no other place from which to peer down and see what she were doing. He ate some dried bird meat while watching her disappear down the shoreline, chewing the flesh slowly with the few yellowed teeth he still had, and when he had finished eating, he smacked his oily lips together, took a long last hungry look, gathered his poles and snares and calabashes, and stealthily disappeared into the forest. A strong hot wind seemed to be gathering; the little birds would be hiding in their nests.

That was in the morning. By evening, the hot sticky wind blew like a fury and the *pili* grass hut could only withstand it because it was situated right up against the vertical cliff walls, in an indentation, almost a cave, in the lava rock. The wind rushed angrily over and around the hut as if it were determined to annihilate it and everything in it. All day it had blown like this, ever since her vision, so that even the kilo, the stargazer and reader of omens, who usually looked upon the wind as a friend, and loved the murmur of both the sea breeze and the whirling sound of the mountain gusts, felt strangely agitated and nervous. Never had she known a searing wind like this, for all the years she had lived here, and she wondered the meaning of it. The wind seemed to be getting into her very bones.

She knew someone was coming to her lonely place, for she had had in the early morning, while resting and staring up at the clouds, an *akaku*, a waking vision. A very large black bird, as big as a man, had flown to the edge of the cliff above her hut, alighted on a tree, and peered down on her. It cocked its head and looked with one eye, and then the other. The black bird had then taken wing from the tree, but instead of soaring high into the sky, it had plummeted to its death on the beach before her hut. She had run to look at it, but when she reached it, it was the white skeleton of the bird, laid out on the sand in a beautiful and intricate pattern of bleached bones. She had stood over the bones, trying to decipher the pattern, for she felt it was a message from the gods, but a small wave had lapped over them; when the wave receded, only white foam remained where the bones had lain. Then she had stirred from the dream. This vision meant death, she knew, but whose death, was a mystery.

In a wild, screeching windstorm like this, there was nothing much she could do. She sat on her haunches in the hut, like an animal, or a primal being, staring through the open doorway at the flying clouds and the silver stars, which shone brilliantly and silently far out at sea, and which were always a comfort to her in this lonely place. She knew somewhat the language of the stars; they spoke to her and made her feel at one with the gods.

Between the gusts of wind, she thought she heard someone calling, but who would come here this night, in this wind? After all these years here, alone, she knew the wind could whisper and could scream with many voices, so she was not afraid. Suddenly though, she knew with a certainty she was not alone.

She wrapped a kapa around her head and went out of the hut. The hot wind blasted into her face. She gazed up at the cliff above her hut; by the light of the stars, she could see that a man was standing above.

"Who are you?" she called up, but her voice was lost in the wind.

The man didn't answer, but disappeared behind the cliff face. She waited for some moments, while the wind howled menacingly all around her. Then the man climbed from above, descending carefully down the crude steps carved in the rock. He stopped before her and stood without speaking; she motioned for him to come in.

Because of the wind, she had no fire. They both sat on the floor in darkness and in silence for a time. At last, she said, "It has been a long time." She moved closer, so that he could hear, for the wind was screaming.

"Yes," he said. "A long time."

Once, a long time ago, they had been lovers, but that was when they were mere children. Now, he was a great chief and he had wives and children of his own. She, however, had chosen to be alone, to be childless, to live here on this wild inlet between two fingers of land that jutted out into the sea, surrounded by impenetrable rocks, so that she could live secluded and undisturbed. Here she practiced her arts, for she had the mark of the gods upon her.

"Why have you come?" she asked. "What do you want with me?"

For a time, he didn't answer. He couldn't see her face or form in the darkness of the hut, so that when he did speak, he felt he was talking to himself, explaining to himself the events that had led him here, to her and to this lonely place.

"I am pursued," he said. "Like the songbird bird flying from the killer hawks, I have had to flee. The king and his chiefs have determined to kill me because I refused to allow my people to pay more tribute. More and more taro, more and more fish, more and more meat, more and more kapas. My people have served me well, and I? I in return have loved them and served them. They are as my children. My people have given everything until they are starving, while the king and his minions have danced and drunk. As the chief of my people, for my people's sake, I have rebelled."

"And have your people followed you?" she asked.

"At first. For my people love me. But after a bitter defeat in battle, with many dead, I was forced to flee. My people protected me for a year, hiding me one place and then another. But now the king has declared he will burn every dwelling, cut every coconut tree, and raze every taro patch in my lands until I am given up. My people are terrified, and will no longer shelter me."

"And now, are you bitter?" she asked.

"I am bitter," he said. "I gave everything for my people. My own children are in great danger. I heard they and their mothers have fled, but where I don't know."

"And who is the object of your bitterness? Your people, who will no longer hide you, or the king and his chiefs, who pursue to kill you?"

He was silent while he thought of this. Then he said, "I am bitter because I will lose my life."

"So," she said, "you are bitter against the gods."

33

He said nothing to this, for he knew better. One must never speak against the gods, though it was true—he was bitter against the gods.

"And now? What will you do now? Where will you go?"

"That is why I have come to you," he answered. "I do not know where to go. Must I live like a dog, hiding in the bushes forevermore? Will you read the omens?"

He was silent again, and then said, "*E kanaaho au ma ka ho'omalu 'ana o kou mau 'eheu*," "I take refuge in the shelter of your wings."

She didn't answer to this, for it had more meaning than she could bear. Instead, after a silence, she said, "Let us rest. Tomorrow we shall talk more, and perhaps read the omens."

She arranged some matting for him apart from her, and he fell asleep immediately, for he hadn't slept for days. She crouched again on her haunches, staring into the darkness. The hot wind blew so that she was uneasy. She gave thought of what she would need for the reading of the omens. And she gave thought to her past with him.

They had loved one another when they were children, but they had always known they could not remain together. He was a high-ranking *ali'i* chief; she was of the kahuna caste, the priestly caste.

Once, when they were playmates, an old man had chastised them for some prank. In jest, she had placed a curse on the old man and he had died in great pain three days later. This had frightened her, this power she held, and after this, she knew she had a special destiny—she was marked as one who would serve the gods. He knew it too. Nevertheless, they had loved one another until he had taken a wife and she had gone away.

They had made love hidden in the green grasses beneath the warm and golden morning sun; they had made love beneath the full moon on the cool sands beside the gentle waves, while listening to the waving, dipping coconut leaves, splashed by sea spray. She had never forgotten the feel of his body against her breast; she had never forgotten the feel of his hair in her fingers. She had loved his hair. His hair was his mana, she had told him. Because of this, he had promised never to cut his hair.

When the last stars had faded, she at last began to feel heavy-eyed. She stretched out on the mat and slept.

In the morning when she awoke, he was gone. The hot wind was still blowing furiously, making her feel agitated and disturbed, as if in the presence of evil, or as if threatened by something malevolent. She came out of her hut and stood in the burning wind with a kapa around her head. The waves of the sea, even in the shelter of the cove, were dashing wildly against each other in every direction, as if they were fighting one another to the death.

From the far end of the isolated cove, where the beach ended against solid unscalable rock, she saw him. He had been in the sea, and he was naked. He saw her and stooped for his malo. Then he walked toward her, and the long black braid of his hair hung to the soles of his feet. He had kept his vow and never cut his hair. He was the finest-looking man she, or anyone, had ever seen.

They ate dried fish and *limu* together, for, as she was a seer, the eating kapu that prohibited men and women from eating together was freed. They ate without speaking, though not in silence, for the hot wind continued to scream and blow about the hut, making it almost impossible to hear one another if they had wanted to speak. After that, he repaired some small nets for her, while she walked the beach of blowing sand, looking up at the wind-swept clouds, searching for omens in the skies.

When she returned to the hut, he said loudly, "What is the meaning of this searing wind?"

She came close and said in his ear, "This is the wind of rage, for there is great anger in the land, and it is a time to be silent. This hot wind will end soon. Tonight we shall have a cold rain. Then we can talk."

She was right, for she knew the way of clouds, the path of the rains, the meaning of the stars, and the language of the gods. In the early evening, the wind stopped all of a sudden in a moment, and the air began to grow cool. At last, they could hear one another.

"Perhaps the king will change his mind after a time," she suggested. "Perhaps he will realize that you are his valuable warrior, and he will call off the pursuit."

"No," he answered, shaking his head, "the king has built a heiau for his god for my sacrifice. He has made an altar for my corpse. He will never call off the pursuit. All his priests, all his warriors, are waiting for my capture. He has given his chiefs the kapu to burn and kill. The burning of the land and the killing of my people has already begun."

She was silent for a while as she saw in her mind's eye the burning of the land and the killing of the people, the innocent men and women and children. She said softly, "Perhaps it is better for one to die than for many to suffer and die."

"Perhaps," he answered with resentment, "but I am not ready to die. I want to live."

She pondered this, for she knew in her belly it was right, that one should die than many. She said, "It is up to the gods, who shall live and who shall die."

"I will live!" he said angrily, and he hit the mat of the floor with his fist. Then his anger subsided, and in an anguished, sorrowful voice he said, "I want to see my children grow. I want to teach my sons. I want to hold my little daughters."

"Listen," she said. "Here comes the rain." And above the cliff, they heard an approaching rustling and then a rumbling, as if a great multitude of people were marching toward and above them. It was the coming of

36

the rain, and while they listened, raindrops began to fall down, at first lightly and sweetly, and then with the intensity of a downpour, and the air became chilly.

She began to make a fire, and while working, she chanted softly. The truth was, he had had to see her again, if even for just one more time. He watched her in silence. She had grown very thin and there was grey in her hair, but her face was fine and beautiful, and she still moved with proud grace. She looked delicate and vulnerable; he knew she was not. Now he felt sorrow because he knew he loved her more than anything, more than his wives, more than his children, more than his lands and his people, but he could never possess her. Watching her, he felt a pity he could not have explained.

"How has it been for you, here alone?" he asked. "Are you not sorry not to have children, a man? Are you not unhappy to sleep alone?"

She continued to work, laying out *ti* leaves in a pattern on the mat, and said, without looking up at him, "It is your attachment to your children, to your wives, to the ones you love, that causes you to be grieved to die. Though I am alone and have no one, I have no grief to die. Those with ought attachment, see clearly. I am a seer."

"Do the bonds of love mean nothing then?" he asked. "Is it not deep love that gives life meaning?"

"To answer that would be to know what love is," she said. She stopped for a moment and gave him a look he did not understand. "Truly," she said, "one way is not the better."

She turned from him and laid out an offering of *'ama'u* fern, and this she sprinkled with salt water and turmeric. All the while, she chanted. He watched her preparations without disturbing her again, for now she was participating in her world, the mythic, numinous world he had no way to enter.

She next took dry *awa* root, sucked it, mixed it with water, sprinkled it with seawater, and drank; in a soft, low voice, she intoned a prayer to her gods. This she repeated until her words began to slur, and her eyes became languid. She lay down before the fire, and dreamt.

At first, she saw images of no meaning, floating bits and pieces of her own consciousness. Then she descended into darkness and silence, and she relaxed into the sleep of the soul.

She was awakened by the sound of many loud voices, incited and arguing, though some were laughing boisterously too. She looked about. There was a crowd of near-naked, animated men—warriors they were, some held long spears high in the air. She could smell the sour odor of their sweating bodies and she sensed their aroused animal passion. Through the chaotic throng, a man was being thrust brutally forward. His arms were tied tightly behind him. His hair hung in a long black braid to the soles of his bare feet. The man was shoved forcibly to the front of the crowd, where he stood with his head erect, looking neither to the left, nor the right, but straight ahead. He was beautiful to look at, with fine-looking, proud features—he was godlike in his handsomeness.

Now an old man, bent with age, and seemingly drunk, came forward, surrounded by various attendants and kahili bearers who were gesturing to one another excitedly. He wore a precious regal cape of crimson and gold feathers, but his skin was scaly and yellow with crust, showing that he was in the habit of drinking much awa. He stood before the captive and his face wore a cruel, indifferent look, showing that he was in the habit of getting his own way.

An attendant blew the *pu*, the sacred triton shell, loud and long three times, and silence came over the throng of men. The crusty old man with the cruel face spoke, and the tone of his voice was pitiless.

"You have dared to rise against me. You have angered the commoners against me, and you have withheld tribute from me. All that is in this land belongs to me!"

There was uproar among the crowd of men, a shouting and stamping of feet.

The old man held his hand up for silence.

"What do you have to say?" he asked of the captive, and he squeezed his face into a hard ball of vindictiveness and his eyes burned with the look of a savage hawk.

The one with bound hands stood looking down upon the old bent man with the cruel demeanor. Courage shone on his face.

"The people must eat," he said, "though the king dances."

"*Pe'e pao*!" the old man shouted, and his face was furious. "Coward! One who hides in caves!"

At this, the man with the long black braid lunged ferociously toward the old man, opening his teeth like a raging dog to grab the old man by the neck, but he was violently knocked to the ground and held by the throng of men.

The old man stumbled backward and then recovered with the help of his attendants. He took a few steps closer and looked down upon the captive held by the crowd. His eyes narrowed, so that, in the feather cape, and with his scaly legs, he looked like an enormous, sick bird of prey.

"Slay him!" he commanded mercilessly, and he turned feebly on his heels, supported by his attendants.

A huge clap of thunder sounded and shook the hut with such force that the dreamer awoke with a start. She looked with unseeing eyes about the hut, and then closed her eyes and descended again into soul sleep.

The corpse of a man was being wrapped carefully in ti leaves. The long braid of his hair was entwined about his neck. She watched as the bundle was slowly cooked over *kukui*-nut shells, in a bed of scorching hot lava stones,

39

like a pig, and she smelled the sickly odor of burning flesh and hair. Then the corpse was unwrapped, and the flesh was like greasy pig. The hair had been seared away. She watched with wonder how the sinewy corpse was burnished with fish oil. The eyes too were anointed with oil, until they shone like the narrowed eyes of a hungry shark.

Then the dreamscape changed and it was nighttime. A throng of silent men stood about gazing up at the glistening corpse, which was made to stand high on a scaffold, the *haka lele*, with a sacrificial spotted pig on one side, and a bending banana stalk, the symbol of submission, on the other. In the darkness, in the gleam of the torch fires, the terrifying corpse glowed as the kahunas, the priests of the god of blood, dressed in feathers and shells, sang their otherworldly chants.

Now the old man with the cruel face, dressed in a magnificent golden-feathered cloak and wearing a crested scarlet-feathered helmet, tottered drunkenly forward, leaning upon attendants, and looked up at the sacrifice. He smiled malignantly, for he enjoyed inspiring fear and terror in the hearts of his chiefs.

What I have done to this one, I can do to you, his smile said, as he looked out among the throng of silent men.

At his signal, another man, a young chief, also dressed in a gold-feathered cloak, stepped forward, took the spotted pig in his arms, and held it toward the altar, while the chanting of the kahunas intensified to a frenzy. Then a giant of a man with a ferocious face, a face like an ax, also wearing a great gold-feathered cloak, stepped abruptly forward and, lifting the gleaming, greasy corpse of the sacrifice in his arms, he held it out as an offering toward the altar.

A brilliant flash of lightening directly overhead suddenly lit up the hut and almost simultaneously, a great peal of thunder sounded and shook the hut and the land itself mightily, so that the dreaming seer opened her eyes momentarily and looked upon the real world without seeing. Then she closed her eyes and drifted down, down, again through darkness and silence and into the sleep of the soul.

When she began to dream again, she saw many curious images. She saw visions of great battles on distant islands, with multitudes of dead and wounded men and women. She saw pictures of strange sailing canoes taller than *koa* trees, and strange men who breathed smoke, and terrible weapons never before known, some that spat fire and stones. She saw multitudes of people felling the great sandalwood trees of the forest, loading them onto the strange canoes, until the sandalwood forests were no more. Then she saw a great king, standing regal, commanding multitudes of warriors, clothed in a magnificent golden-feathered cloak, and she recognized him as the ferocious giant with the face like an ax who had offered the greasy corpse. Then she saw this same giant of a man old and on his deathbed, and she heard the words he was saying.

After that, she saw many more strange, bewildering images, which she struggled to look closely at, to understand, but an incessant soft pounding bothered her, to which she found herself listening, and she began to float up and up, until at last she surfaced, and opened her eyes drowsily to a more familiar world. She stared at the dying embers of a fire. The rain was pounding.

For a long time she lay on her side without stirring, looking into the red embers, seeing the dreams again in her mind's eye. It was not that she did not understand the portents, but could the will of the gods be changed? Could destiny be changed? How much dare she entangle herself with the gods' commands?

41

After a long while, she rolled to her side and sat up, without looking at the man who was sitting watching her. She stirred the embers and fed the fire with some sticks.

Then she turned and faced the man.

"Am I to die?" he asked.

"We all die," she answered, without emotion.

"Yes, we all die," he said, "but am I to die now, hunted down like a pig, and slain for a sacrifice to the gods?"

She looked at him in silence for a time before answering. Then she turned her back to him and stared into the fire.

"You shall live," she said. "You shall not be offered like a pig. Let us rest now."

He lay down and fell asleep quickly and deeply, for his mind was at ease. She, however, lay awake, restless and uneasy, until at last she rose and stood in the door of the hut, feeling the cold wind of the rain. Far out on the sea, the stars were shining bright.

Why am I not rain, or wind, instead of this being in a woman's skin? she wondered. Why am I not a wave of the sea, or starlight?

She looked toward him, and he awoke and saw her silhouetted against the opening of the hut.

"Come," he said, softly, and he held his arms out to enfold her. "The night is cold, and my belly is warm. It is not good to sleep alone."

She went to him then, and lay beside him and wrapped her arms around his neck, and they clung together in the thrill of love, in the fragrance of love, their thighs rejoicing.

By dawn, the rain had stopped and when she awoke, he was not there. When she walked outside her hut, he was coming from the far end of the cove, with two sparkling fish in his hands.

"I will make you a fine meal," he said to her, with a smile on his face.

She smiled also, for it was good to see him light-hearted, and she felt joy, which she had not felt for many years.

The morning passed while they both worked on repairing the hut. They went together up the cliff and into the forest to gather wood and vines. When the sun was high in the sky, they sat together on a rock overlooking the sea.

"You must remain in hiding," she said, which was the first time she had spoken again of the portents. "You can remain here, in this lonely place. The king shall die one day."

"I will remain here," he answered. "There are many ways I can help you. There is much a man can do for a woman." He laughed when he said this, and his eyes twinkled. Then he said, "I shall fatten you," and he picked up her thin hand and held it.

She laughed too, and the sound of her own laughter surprised her, for she had not heard it in many years.

"That is good," she said. "No one comes here, so you shall be safe as long as you remain."

"It will not be so unpleasant to live alone with you here," he said, and his eyes shone. "*E kanaaho au ma ka ho'omalu 'ana o kou mau 'eheu*," "I take refuge in the shelter of your wings."

She laughed again, for long ago, in days past, when they had been lovers, he had called her "little bird." But then she had an afterthought.

"At times," she said, "the bird catcher wanders in the forests above. Beware of him. You must take care and not be seen."

"I am a warrior; I am stealthier than a bird catcher," he said, and his eyes smiled with cheerfulness. *Pe'epe'e pueo*. I shall hide like an owl in a tree."

"Take care," she said and laughed, "the crafty bird catcher sometimes gets the day-sleeping owl."

The days passed pleasantly for the seer and the long-haired chief. Indeed, he did fatten her with the big fish he caught from the sea. And she was happy to share the seaweeds and mollusks she gathered. He carried water from the stream in the forest, brought wood, hunted for pigs in the forest, and made himself useful in many ways. In a short time, they became accustomed to their life together, apart from the world of men and women, as if they had always been alone together.

*

One evening he was quieter than usual. He sat staring into the fire.

"Why the sorrowful face?" she asked. "Have you become weary with my company?"

"I am thinking of my people," he said, "of my children."

She said nothing at first, for she felt his grief. But then she had a thought.

"It is the season for the bird catcher to be about," she said. "I could walk about in the forest and perhaps find him. He will have news."

With this in mind, the next day she climbed the cliff carrying her calabash, and headed in the direction of the bird catcher's hut. In the afternoon, just before reaching his hut, she met him as he was returning from setting his snares. He was greatly surprised to see her, though he did not say it.

He looked at her curiously, for he was expert at sizing up the bodies of birds, whether thin or thick. It seemed to him that she had grown fatter and stronger. But he said nothing about this.

She smiled at him as she had once smiled. He, sharp as he was, was immediately suspicious. She took her calabash from her shoulder, and offered him some dried seaweed.

"I am gathering mushrooms," she said affably, and she showed him what she had gathered.

As she had given him the seaweed, he took some bits of dried bird meat from his calabash to give to her. While he did this, she sat down nearby, as though she would stay awhile.

"What news do you have of the world, bird catcher?" she asked.

So! he thought, she has grown lonely, for there was no other reason for her to have wandered so far as the door of his hut.

He told her first of the good birding season, of the many *'o'o* and *'i'iwi* and *'apapane* and other birds he had caught. He saw from looking at her from the corner of his eyes that she seemed to be listening with great interest. It occurred to him, shrewd as he was, that she had come for some of the crimson or gold feathers for herself. He determined within himself that he would offer her none.

"The king must be very pleased with you," she said, "for he shall have many new feathered cloaks."

The bird catcher knew she was flattering him, but still he succumbed to her praise.

"The king is always pleased with Halulu," the bird catcher boasted, "for no other bird catcher has brought him such an abundance of crimson and gold wing feathers and tail feathers. He has told me so himself."

He spat on the ground after saying this, then wiped his mouth with the back of his hand, and smiled with a smile that suggested he was on the best of terms with the king, indeed, that he was one of the king's favorites.

"That is good," she said, and she smiled in a friendly fashion. "And the king? How is our king?"

"The king is well," answered the bird catcher, and he spat on the ground again. "He is happy to have me for his bird catcher," he added smugly, for he relished her praise.

As he said nothing more regarding the king, she said, "And our people? What news do you have of our people?"

He told her then news concerning the people he had met in his wanderings. She asked him questions in an attempt to lead him to what she most wanted to know, and when he failed to give her the news she wanted, she became frustrated.

"Is the king burning the precious land of some of the people?" she asked directly.

Now, the bird catcher, quick-witted as he was, instantly perceived the frustration in her voice, and how she shifted uneasily when she asked this, and how her smile quickly changed into a frown.

And how would she know of the burning of the land? he thought to himself, but his own face did not betray his thoughts, for he was adept at concealment.

"Ah!" said the bird catcher. "You speak of that rebel chief who has tripped one foot over another! It is true. The king has given to the god of his high chiefs the burning of that rebel's land, from the uplands to the sea, because he has refused to lay tribute on the altar of the king."

"Why should the king burn the land?" she asked further.

"The king wants the life of that long-haired chief, and he has vowed to cut that haughty chief's hair with the shark's-tooth knife!" The bird catcher laughed. "He has built a heiau for his sacrifice when that rebel should be taken. Because that chief is beloved by his people, the people were hiding him. But now that chief will roast like a spotted pig."

"And now what of the rebel's people?" she asked.

"The houses of the people are being burned," he replied. "The taro fields, the coconut and banana trees are being destroyed. Many people have fled, and some have died. The king has sworn that the burning will not stop until that rebel is found."

"I am sorry for those people," she murmured, looking down at the ground.

The bird catcher shrugged and said nothing to this, but only stood and scratched his crotch, for he cared not at all for the burning of the land or what happened to the people.

She rose to her feet abruptly.

"I must go now, for it shall soon enough be dark," she said.

The bird catcher was surprised at her sudden end to their conversation; he had flattered himself that she had come to see him. In an attempt to entice her to stay with him, he plucked two feathers from his calabash, a crimson feather and a gold feather, and held them toward her invitingly. He said nothing but his mouth twisted in an ugly, lewd smile.

"O my friend," she said, "I thank you, but I would not for anything put at risk your great friendship with the king."

With these words, and a wave of her hand, she turned and walked briskly back from the direction in which she had come.

He watched her go with sullen resentment, for somehow, he felt himself tricked. The thought of forcing her to his will came to his mind, but then he remembered how her eyes could flash fire. He watched her until she was out of sight in the shadows of the trees, and even after she was gone, he didn't turn toward his hut. He took from his calabash two delicate bird eggs, wrapped carefully in fern leaves, and he plopped them into his mouth, one after the other, and he stood there, just thinking.

Just at evening time, she arrived at the cliff over the cove, but she stopped before descending the crude steps. An enormous purplish-blue cloud, the color of a bad bruise, hung low in the sky just off shore, though not another cloud of any color was to be seen. She stood staring at it, wondering at the meaning of it, and a feeling of unease came over her, but then movement below caught her eye and she looked down on her hut and the beach.

She saw the one she loved running toward the far end of the beach. She stood and watched him as he turned and then dashed at full speed toward the opposite end of the cove. He had loosed his long braid and as he ran, his black shiny hair flew behind him. He was tall and sleek, and ran fast with long strides. Truly, she thought, he looks like a god. She started down the steps.

He was at the far end of the cove when he saw her. She walked toward the water to meet him, still carrying her calabashes, and stood at the water's edge, wetting her feet. As he ran toward her, his body glistened with his sweat. He stopped before her, took the calabashes from her hands, and set them on the sand. Then he embraced her and touched his nose to her nose.

"*A'o no I ke koa, a a'o pu no ho'I I ka holo.*" "When one learns to be a warrior one must also learn to run," he said, catching his breath, and smiling. "So my teachers have taught me."

She smiled back and pointed to the calabashes. "Just look," she said, "there are many mushrooms in the forest now."

"And the bird catcher?" he asked eagerly.

"Yes," she answered. "I have seen the bird catcher."

"And what news?" he asked, and his face turned grim.

"It is as you have said," she answered, smiling up at him. "The king is determined to roast you."

48

She hesitated for a moment, looking into his face. Then she looked up at the bruise-colored cloud, which still hung in the sky.

"But," she said, "I have good news also. The chiefs have left off burning the land and killing the people, and your wives and children are safe."

Tears came into his eyes, and he embraced her, lifting her off the ground, and touching his nose to her nose again. He released her and bent to carry the calabashes.

"Wait!" she said playfully. "The bird catcher has sent you a little present of dried bird meat." She put her hand into the calabash and pulled out the leaf-wrapped meat. She unwrapped the green leaves, and held the dried bird meat to his nose.

"We shall feast tonight," she said, with a smile.

He sniffed the bird meat.

"You must thank my friend the bird catcher for me," he said, and he chuckled.

"Yes," I will," she answered, laughing. "When I see him next." And she pursed her lips and whistled the lovely mating call of the *manu-o-Ku*, the white love-tern, which made him smile. Then they each picked up a calabash, and walked to the hut, holding hands.

From up on that cliff, above the hut, two beady black eyes watched them, until they entered the hut and could be seen no more.

"Aha!" murmured the bird catcher, as he stood and munched on the dried wing of an owl. "This songbird is snared and will soon be plucked of his fine feathers."

He picked a twig from a bush nearby, and began to pick his teeth while he speculated to himself on his reward.

Perhaps the king will give me one of his fine daughters, or a large piece of land with plenty food and a servant to cook it, or both, he conjectured, so that I never again must wander about hunting birds in the rainy and cold forests.

He turned this thought about in his mind while he turned the twig in the gaps between his yellowed teeth, but in a few moments, he discarded the notion, for, after all, he was one man who relished his work.

He spat and then wiped the drool from his mouth with the back of his hand, gathered his poles and snares, and ambled away into a quickly darkening and threatening forest. Spirits would soon be about, under the coverings of the wings of night, but that was fine, for he knew his way about in the dark as well as the short-eared owl. He laughed gleefully to himself as he went along; in fact, he felt in such high spirits, he decided to spend the night robbing nests.

*

Some days passed after her visit to the bird catcher. One morning she awoke to a fine misty rain and found herself alone, which was not unusual, for her rebel lover often slipped away early now to hunt pigs in the forest. She knew by the warmth of the coverings that he had only just departed, and she lay for a while in the comfort of his warmness, listening to the light raindrops. By the time she arose and put on her kapa, the rain had stopped.

She looked out from the doorway to the beach, and was astonished to see in the brilliant morning sunlight a rainbow of only three colors, yellow, red and green, stretched out directly from end of the cove to the other, so close that it seemed she could walk into it. She wished he were here to see something so beautiful and rare as this. She hurriedly stepped from the hut, and walked to one end of the beach, but when she reached the end of the rainbow, it was no longer there.

She wandered along the beach in the morning, picking seaweed, and spreading it out in the sun on a rock to dry. She would glance toward the hut every now and then, thinking that perhaps he would be descending the carved steps, but when the sun was high in the sky, he still had not returned. In the hot afternoon, she bathed in the sea, and combed her hair and then rubbed her skin with coconut oil until it shone. She kept thinking that at any moment, he would be climbing down the cliff, but when evening came, and he had not returned, she scaled the carved steps to the top of the overhang and stood peering into the forest until it was too dark to see. After that, she returned to the hut and began to make a fire.

When darkness settled, she did not eat, but sat before the fire. She pondered the meaning of the morning rainbow, for she had never seen a rainbow of only three colors. She knew that such a strange apparition portended death. She listened for the sound of footsteps, and after many hours had passed, and the fire had died, she walked out upon the beach. There was no moon, no stars; the night was swathed in blackness.

It is possible, she thought, that he has fallen into a *puka*, a lava crevice, for there were many such places, covered over by jungle vines and ferns, hidden until an unwary traveler stepped into one and fell into the hole, perhaps becoming trapped or breaking bones.

At last, she reentered her hut, and lay down upon the mat, but it was a long time before she drifted into an uneasy sleep.

She awoke at the first light of morning, and at first, she didn't remember why she felt so troubled. When she remembered, she quickly rose, gathered her calabashes, and climbed the steps to the forest. She first went in the direction she thought he might have taken. She walked along, sometimes calling his name, sometimes just listening.

Morning and noon and afternoon passed and she began to retrace her steps. The forest was beginning to darken very quickly when she neared the cliff over her hut.

51

As she approached, something on the dark ground caught her eye. It was a golden feather.

She stooped to pick it up and she looked at it very thoughtfully. Then she parted the low bushes that were within reach, and saw upon the ground tiny tidbits of blue eggshells littering the earth.

The bird catcher has been here, she thought, and she gazed out over the top of her hut onto the beach, from one end of the cove to the other. The last golden rays of sunlight were illuminating the sand and the waves, but no one was to be seen, nor were there footprints upon the sand. She waited and watched.

As I wait and watch, so has the bird catcher, she reflected uneasily, and she brushed her cheek with the back of the feather, and frowned. Then she descended the cliff and entered her hut. She stuck the golden feather in the straw wall over her sleeping mat.

She did not make a fire, nor did she eat. She lay on her mat, her mind disturbed. In the morning, she again rose early, gathered her calabashes, and searched for the one she loved in another direction.

At the end of the third day of searching, at times calling softly for him, she returned when the blue shadows of the trees lengthened and it would soon be too dark to see. She stopped at the top of the cliff and parted the bushes. There among twigs and leaves lay tiny white bones. She picked them up and held them in her palm.

She descended the steps to her hut, carrying delicate bones in her hand, and because a cold rain had begun to fall, she made a fire and sat before it. She had searched the forest far in all directions; if he had been hurt, she would have found him.

She thought about the bird catcher, and the tiny bones found in the bushes. Then she thought on her love.

She refused, at first, to allow herself to think that evil had befallen him. He is stealthier than the stupid bird catcher, she reassured herself. He said so himself. No, he has gone to find his wives and children.

She set about to make an offering to the gods for his safety, and when she had finished chanting her soul's desire, she sat before the fire long into the night. She recalled every detail of the omens she had dreamed for him, when he had first come here.

I have tried to outwit the gods, she thought. I have tried to change destiny, and now I am punished for my love of him. It were better that I had not loved him.

She lay down on her mat, and her last thought, before drifting off into sleep, was that, perhaps, one day, he would return.

*

One morning, some time later, she set out to find the bird catcher. She placed the gold feather in one of the calabashes she carried. She climbed the cliff and walked to his hunting grounds. She found him sitting in a clearing, repairing a large net. He was sucking on a bone.

His eyes met hers as she approached him, but he quickly looked down again, a wily smile playing about his thick lips.

She has grown thin again, thought the bird catcher, and the thought made him feel happy and triumphant.

"Good day, bird catcher," she said, in greeting, but she did not smile.

"Good day," murmured the bird catcher, without looking up at her.

She reached into her calabash and took out the gold feather.

"I found this on the path," she said. "On the path near my hut."

She held it between two fingers, and then let it go; the gold feather fluttered to the bird catcher's feet.

He saw it, but still did not look up at her. Instead, he spat out the bone he had been sucking on.

"And how goes the birding?" she asked, standing before him.

"The birding goes well," said the bird catcher, still without looking up. "The king is well pleased with the birds I have caught for him. Very well pleased indeed! See this net I am mending?"

Now the bird catcher looked up at her with a glint in his eye. "With this net such a grand bird I have caught for the king! Delivered to him unblemished too! Yes, not a mark on him!"

"Well for you," she said, and a river of anger began to rise in her. "And what news have you?"

"I have good news," he said with a chuckle. "I have news of that long-haired rebel, the one the king vowed to roast."

The bird catcher rose to his feet, holding the net. He spat to the side, and then looked her straight in the eyes.

"That song bird has been snared and plucked of his feathers," said the bird catcher, and he giggled. "Yes, roasted and oiled and sacrificed between a spotted pig and a banana stalk."

The bird catcher's mouth contorted into an ugly grin, while he stared into her eyes.

"A pity," said the bird catcher, smirking. "Such a handsome bird to warm the nest at night. Some lady bird will miss his black down against her soft breast."

The bird catcher cackled until thick drool stood on his chin. She stood staring back at him for a long moment, and it seemed to her that the earth shook.

He stopped cackling and wiped the slobber from his chin with the back of his hand, and then he narrowed his eyes and looked into hers.

"I have something for you," he said, and his eyes were bright and sly. "Something the king gave me."

He stooped and fished about in his calabash. Then he brought out something wrapped in a green leaf.

"For you," he said. "A little gift from my friend the king."

He unwrapped the leaf and held up between his thumb and his forefinger a fishhook made of human bone.

She stood as though turned to stone.

"For you," the bird catcher said again, and he cavalierly dropped the bone into her calabash, threw his net across his shoulders and stooped to gather his calabash and poles. He stood and slung his calabash across his back, gazing into her eyes exultantly. Then he hooted with laughter, turned, and walked away.

"Good morning!" he crowed over his shoulder, and he whistled gaily as he disappeared into the forest.

For some time she remained standing without moving, staring at the ground where the golden feather still lay. At last, she stooped to retrieve it, and she picked up the bone remnants upon which the bird catcher had gnawed. These she placed into her calabash, and she slowly, slowly began the walk back to her hut, clutching tightly the fishhook made of human bone.

*

For a day and a night, after returning to her cove, she sat on the big rock overlooking the waves, just watching the sea. She wished she could weep and wail, as was the custom of her people in expressing grief, but she could not. She could not shed a single tear. She merely sat and clutched the fishhook made of the bone of her love.

She could not help but wonder if the fishhook were made of his arm bone or his leg bone. She held it up in the light of the sun, and she could see that it was skillfully carved; it was as smooth and polished as the sea stones that wash up and down in the waves.

She held the fishhook against the naked skin of her belly, closed her eyes and listened. She heard his voice at once.

"Is it not deep love that gives life meaning?" he said again. "Do the bonds of love mean nothing?"

When she had finished listening, she opened her eyes and stared at the waves of the sea. Then she pursed her lips, and began to whistle.

*

In the evening, she wrapped the golden feather and the bones on which the bird catcher had sucked in a ti leaf. These she sprinkled with seawater and turmeric and tossed into the fire. After that, she chanted to the bird god—the very chant the bird catcher had taught her—and then she prayed and asked for a boon.

"O Ku-huluhulu-manu," she prayed," for one night only, give me the eyes of the short-eared owl that I may move about in the shadows of the forest, under the coverings of the wings of night, like a night spirit, unseen but not unheard, and give me a song so compelling a man's bones will ache."

Then she lay down on her mat to take rest, with the fishhook made from the bones of her love resting on her belly.

*

Some hours before dawn, when the day birds lay asleep in their nests, their little ones between them dreaming, and the night spirits wandered the forest, she rose. She hung the fishhook made from the bone of her love on a plaited vine and this she placed around her neck. Without gathering her calabashes, she left her hut, climbed to the top of the cliff, and made her way through the forest toward the bird catcher's hut. She walked quickly and silently, so that even the little birds dreaming in their nests did not hear.

When she neared his hut, close but not too close, she stood behind a tree and caught her breath. In the branches above, an owl ruffled his feathers and stared down at her, perplexed.

She filled her lungs with air, and then, at first very softly, began to whistle a song so exquisitely lovely, that the bird catcher, asleep in his hut, awoke thrilled. She paused, and then whistled again. The third time she whistled, the dark shape of the bird catcher emerged from his hut. She could see even in the darkness how he cocked his head to one side to listen. She whistled again, very softly, while the owl in the branches above blinked and stared.

The dark shape of the bird catcher began to walk toward her, so that she turned and ran with unheard footsteps under the coverings of the wings of night, and hid behind another tree. She whistled somewhat louder, and after some minutes, the dark shape of the bird catcher could be seen coming in her direction. She saw him stop and cock his head, listening.

Again she ran quickly and lightly through the forest, and hid in the blue shadows. She whistled this time long and long, and after a few moments, the shape of the bird catcher came toward her.

In this way, she lured the bird catcher through the forest. Just before the first light of dawn, and the folding of the wings of night, she had enticed him almost to the top of the cliff that overhung her hut.

She stopped then, and stood behind a tree, watching. Just as she had expected, he walked to the cliff edge, and peered down upon her hut. He stood spying down and she stealthily crept forward from the shadows. With one mighty shove, she pushed him over the edge. His arms flapped and waved, his hands tore at the air, and he cawed like a felled black bird as he plunged to the beach below.

She walked without hurry down the steps to where he had fallen in the damp sand. He lay on his broken back like a dying bird, his arms and legs splayed out and twitching; from his throat came a peculiar clucking sound. His neck was twisted grotesquely, the feathers he wore in his hair were bent and crooked, and his hands were beginning to curl like dying claws.

She looked down on him and said, "You. Halulu. You were named for the magic bird whose feathers are made of water particles from the dazzling orb of the sun, whose every feather is tipped by a tearing talon, but now your flesh will rot till it is black and your bones shall bleach white by that same sun."

Then she removed the fishhook from around her neck, held it to her belly, and listened to the voice of the one she loved.

"Come," he said so tenderly, "the night is cold, my belly is warm. It is not good to sleep alone."

Then she turned and walked into the warm arms of the sea.

BROKEN VOW

Her portrait, in its original mid-eighteenth-century oval frame, hung all but neglected in her great, great, great granddaughter's beach house on Kealakekua Bay, a multi-million dollar ocean-front real estate property much coveted as a "listing" by greedy-eyed realtors. Few people noticed the portrait, and fewer still commented on it— somehow the dusky lady it depicted seemed forlornly out of place, obsolete—a shadowy sadness somehow interjected from more than a century past into the happy, endless summer of surfing and kayaking, snorkeling and string bikinis, tanning oil and smoothies and wine coolers. At first glance, though dressed in the highest fashion of Victorian finery, with great hat and gloves, the dark lady seemed homely and not of particular interest. Sometimes someone might glance up and casually ask, "Who's that?" and the answer was "A great, great, great Hawaiian ancestor." Then sometimes, if any interest were further expressed, the aged and ragged kahili, the feather standard which had once been the lady's standard of royalty but was now not much more than some sticks with a few dusty falling feathers, was also pointed out, but rarely did anyone ask anything more or examine the portrait more carefully.

But if one did take a closer look, the portrait seemed to reveal a story, and the dark lady became fascinating. One sensed, from the way the lady held her hands, stiff and posed, that she was acutely uncomfortable. It was more than that she was a very brown native *wahine* dressed in the nineteenth-century stylish finery of the very white lady that made her seem out of place, unnatural, and even somewhat pathetic, as if she were trying to be what she was not. It was more than her dark, inscrutable eyes and unsmiling face. When one looked more carefully, one could see that actually she was a great beauty. If only somehow she could doff the hat and gloves and high-collared, starched, ornamented dress of the Victorian haole woman, the white lady, and instead drape herself in the simple and graceful tapa cloth that the wahine, the women of her people, had worn for centuries. If only she could remove the overly-ornate comb in her hair, and the ludicrous hat from her head, and let down her dark, luxurious tresses; yes, then one could see that the dark lady indeed was extraordinarily, exotically, beautiful.

Her name was Kilia, and she was a Maui highborn chiefess, and there was a little-known legend about her. It was said that she protected those who sailed the Alenuiha'ha Channel from Hawaii to Maui from fear.

Betrothed almost at birth by a family *ho'opalau*, a vow, to an ali'i chief many years older, Kilia had lived the privileged childhood befitting her royal station. Born less than two decades after the great events of 1819—the death of the peerless king, the breaking of the kapus and the overthrow of the old order and the old gods, the arrival of the missionaries with their new god—she had yet been brought up in the old ways by an ali'i family that, secretly and faithfully, still made offerings to the *akua* and *'aumakua*, the gods and the family gods.

As befitting a royal *keikamahine*, an ali'i girl-child born to the lineage of the great kings of Hana, the ancient prescriptions for creating a beautiful and graceful wahine worthy of a chief were followed with exactitude; even as an infant, customs were followed with an eye to the child becoming an appealing sexual mate. Her privates were

60

massaged and molded with milk and kukui nut oil, while *meles*, songs to honor her genealogy, past and future, were chanted. Meles were even chanted to her genitals. Her person had been made kapu, forbidden to men upon pain of death, to insure her virginity until she joined her royal chief on the sleeping mat, when she should come of age, which meant when her menses began. Until then, she was trained in the graces and manners that an ali'i chiefess of high station should possess, including the arts of lovemaking. Kilia had her own servants; work never touched her hands. She spent her days happily idle, bathing in the streams, playing with whatever amused her.

As was customary among the royal ancients, Kilia was adopted, *hanai'd*, in infancy, by a great uncle, and this uncle hated the haoles, the whites, and despised those who no longer honored the gods of old. In the isolation of Hana, this chief and others continued to uphold the time-honored traditions of the ancestors, in spite of Kamehameha II's abolishment of the kapus and his decree imposing the destruction of the sacred temples. Kilia had been sheltered from the loathed influence of the missionary people who had begun to arrive in 1820; she lived still in the old time of the ancient islanders.

Kilia was now just in her early teens; her legs were long and shapely, her breasts were budding. Her thick hair was black as night and fell to her thighs. Her face was lovely to look upon. With the graces in which she had been trained, Kilia was indeed a prize. Her beauty was spoken of far and wide, and was already the stuff of legend making, for Hawaiians love to immortalize beautiful women.

Now that she had entered puberty, her marriage to the chief her betrothed was being planned. Kilia neither looked forward to this event, nor did she dread it. It was simply the role that she had been taught to play her whole life. Childhood had just ended; now her high destiny was

61

to bear royal descendants to her chief, for the good of the people and the land. This was all according to the old ways.

One night at the time of full moon, she had a dream that seemed both wondrous and disturbing. She went to a *wehewehe moe 'uhane*, a dream interpreter, who understood these things.

The dream interpreter listened carefully, and then said, "This dreams means that things shall not be as they were meant to be. This dream means two things: you shall have great happiness, above all riches, but it also means you shall suffer great sorrow, beyond all bearing."

"Which shall come first?" Kilia asked.

"The happiness shall come first," answered the dream interpreter. "And then the sorrow."

"Tell me," said Kilia, "who sends this dream to me?"

"This revelation of the night, *ho'ike na ka po*, it comes from the ancestors, the 'aumakua.'"

Kilia sat in thought for a few moments, and then rose to go.

"One thing more," said the wehewehe moe 'uhane, and she looked at Kilia searchingly.

"What is that?" Kilia asked.

"For your sake, you should tell this dream to no one."

Kilia nodded and departed.

About this same time, during this same full moon, as destiny would have it—for things were not to be as they were meant to be—on the island of Hawaii, one handsome young Ebenezer Parker was hearing of this great beauty of Hana. Just twenty years old, he was the second son of John Palmer Parker. John Palmer Parker himself had been in his early twenties, when, jumping ship and remaining on Hawaii Island when his ship set sail, he was befriended by the great King Kamehameha I.

Eventually the King, the conqueror of all the islands, gave him to wed his sixteen-year-old granddaughter, princess Keliikipakaneokaolohaka; along with her came six hundred acres of prime land in Kohala as a dowry, and the special privilege of being the only man allowed to hunt the King's wild cattle which ran wild on Hawaii. Kipakane, the royal princess, was renamed Rachel by the Christian John Palmer Parker, and she bore him three children. John Palmer Parker prospered, as they who are favored by kings do, eventually building a Cape Cod-style home for his native wife and *hapa-haole*, half-white, children, and creating the Parker dynasty and wealth that was to endure for generations as the great Parker Ranch.

Rachel, Kipikane, brought with her to Kohala her lifestyle as an ali'i. Those who had served her for a lifetime accompanied her, and as in the old way, attended her and her family. In the beginning, for the first three years of their marriage, while King Kamehameha I still lived, the old ways were followed. Kipikane and her women servants ate separately from the men in the *hale 'aina*, the women's eating house, and ate only those foods allowed to women. But in 1819, upon the death of the King, the kapus were abolished, the temples overthrown, and the ancient gods abandoned. Kipikane, at first hesitant, began to have her meals with her husband.

From the beginning then, this family was unique in all the islands. The royal blood line in itself commanded deference from all the native people; added to this, the very special status of haole John Palmer Parker as a minion of the King commanded the highest respect from both chiefs and commoners alike. The three children of John Palmer and Kipikane were considered ali'i, of royal blood. It was said throughout the islands that John Palmer Parker had great mana, supernatural power.

John Palmer Parker didn't believe in mana; he was a down-to-earth fundamentalist Christian sailor who understood that he who has might has right. And what he had had to command the respect of King Kamehameha I was a state-of-the-art musket. Perhaps he loved Kipakane, but more importantly, a man needed a helpmate and a bearer of his children, according to the Holy Bible. Rachel's Hawaiian ways were neither frowned upon nor overlooked by John Palmer. They were just accepted as part and parcel of being the lot of a sailor who had jumped ship and was making a home in the islands, had befriended a king and won his granddaughter. John Palmer Parker was lucky and he knew it.

The three children, Mary, John Parker II, and Ebenezer, thus grew up at the confluence of two very different cultures. From mother Kipikane and the servants, the children learned Hawaiian and the Hawaiian ways; from father John Palmer, they learned English and the ways of the haoles. Attended to and pampered by native servants, but without the discipline provided by the males of the traditional Hawaiian ohana, the children were somewhat spoiled and willful. This was, fortunately, tempered by John Palmer Parker's practicality and Christian philosophy that the rod should not spareth the child. For John Palmer Parker was a devout Christian. Though outwardly he showed respect to the natives and their ways, in fact he looked upon them as naive and heathen and regarded many of their customs as superstitious fantasy, imposed upon them by kahunas, witch doctors, who through fear subjugated the common people.

Samuel, the eldest son, inherited his father's practicality. When he fell in love with a commoner, and decided to wed her, he was the talk of the natives, who viewed the marriage of royalty and commoner as a disgrace and doomed. Samuel didn't care, and his wife Hanai, beautiful and shy, held her head high with modest pride, but always remembering her station. Chiefess Kipikane was opposed to this marriage, but father John Palmer Parker had the last word. How could he oppose such a union, based on caste? He himself had no royal lines, yet he had married a chiefess. So he gave his blessing. Kipikane, true to her aristocratic upbringing, bore this indignity with noble graciousness, and was kind to Hanai. It was whispered that such a marriage would be barren; in fact, Samuel and Hanai bore only one child, a son, who died at only one year of age.

It was Ebenezer, the younger son, who took full advantage of his high and lucky station in life. Blessed with exceedingly good looks, he was fair skinned, with black hair and black eyes. He dressed haole style in the latest fashions from Honolulu. Among barefooted-natives, he strode about like an otherworldly prince in expensive polished boots and silver-plated spurs. Besides being a skillful horseman, and the wealthiest young man around, he had charisma. And he loved the fair sex. Every native girl for whom he had lusted, and there had been many, had succumbed to his charms. Yet he himself had never felt the pangs and joys of true love. He walked about with a swagger that indicated he was, above all, quite in love with himself.

So when the rumor reached him that full-moon night that the most beautiful virgin in all of the Hawaiian Islands lived in Hana, he resolved to go there and see for himself. Relying not only on his charm, good looks, new clothes for the occasion, and prestige, he took along a few gifts with which to woo her— a lovely piece of white silk, a brass hand-mirror, a porcelain locket—for the native girls loved trinkets. He departed for Maui on the pretext of business.

Once in Hana, it was easy to find a native to lead him to Kilia's ohana. Early one morning, three days after Kilia had dreamed her dream of the future, the guide stood in the trees and pointed out the *kulanakauhale*, the family compound, to Ebenezer. Ebenezer looked exotically handsome in his haole finery—his wide-brimmed felt hat, buttoned shirt, polished boots, silver-plated spurs. He strode confidently forward, relying on his charm, and the ubiquitous Hawaiian hospitality toward strangers, to gain him entrance to the family compound.

As fortune would have it, Kilia was alone with two attendants who were combing her long black hair. And as luck would have it, and Ebenezer always had good luck, the *kane*, the men of the ohana, were away for the day on a pig hunt. Kilia had just taken her morning bath, and her skin shone like warm gold in the morning light. He saw her before she saw him. Taken aback by her great loveliness, and the graceful way she sat on her mat with her knees pulled in, native style, he stood stock still and just stared at her. She was as beautiful as had been told, and more so. His eyes took in the whole scene, life being lived the ancient royal aristocratic way. Suddenly, and for the first time in his life, he felt ashamed. What was he doing here, dressed like a silly dandy with his trinkets for gifts? He knew what he was here for, and his face turned red. He turned to go.

Just at that moment, Kilia spotted him.

"*E komo mai*," she innocently called to him. "Welcome, stranger."

He turned around and looked back at her, hesitant.

Again she called, "Come, enter."

It was not long before he was sitting on her tapa mat, and the two were talking and laughing. The attendants were shocked, and sat at a distance, watching fearfully, for themselves and Kilia. When they saw Kilia repose backward, arch her back and smile, and the stranger bend over her budding breasts while she giggled, they looked at one another with alarm. So the morning passed, with Ebenezer and Kilia lost in joy, laughing and chattering, like reunited brother and sister, until Kilia called to her servants to bring food.

The servants reluctantly brought poi, and placed before Kilia her calabash. For the strange guest, they placed another calabash.

"Shall we eat?" said Kilia, and she offered her calabash to Ebenezer. The two ate from the one calabash. Thus, to the horror of the two attendants, Kilia offered herself to Ebenezer. For there was only one meaning when a man and a woman ate from the same bowl.

"Surely she will be dreadfully punished," the two servants whispered to one another.

Before the afternoon sun was high in the sky, Ebenezer knew. He had really known from the moment he had first seen her—she was the one. His heart was smitten. Never before had he felt *ahi wele*, love hot as fire. Accustomed to getting his way whenever he wished, he did not hesitate to ask her to wed him.

For the first time all day, Kilia frowned.

"I am betrothed," she answered, "and before many days have passed, I shall be married to a high chief."

Undaunted, Ebenezer laid before her how much more he had to offer, including how much higher his own station in life was.

"My father was the friend of King Kamehameha I," he boasted less than subtly. "My mother is the grand-daughter of the greatest king that has ever lived. I myself am a Kamehameha."

Still Kilia frowned, for, for the first time all day, she remembered the dream.

"An *'olelo pa'a* is a binding vow," she said. "From since time began, it is known that a vow must never be broken."

"But you never promised to marry," Ebenezer argued convincingly.

"No, but my father, my uncle, my ohana, have promised, and that is even a more powerful vow. It would not be *pono*, it would be wrong, to break the vow."

"The old ways are gone," replied Ebenezer confidently, with a dismissing wave of his hand. "What was once *pono 'ole*, what was once wrongdoing, is no longer. What matters now is that you and I are in love. The old ways are gone. The new way is that we must be happy. We are meant to be together. We are meant to be happy."

For Ebenezer had no doubt. And he laid before Kilia the vision of the new way, life with him on the ranch at Kohala, and the golden happiness of a future together.

In the late afternoon, in the declining yellow light, the watchful attendants saw Ebenezer take a beautiful strip of white silk and tear it down the middle. One-half he gave to Kilia; when she stood, he wrapped it around her waist; the other he folded into his travel bag. To the attendants, he gave the trinkets that were unworthy of his love, the locket and the mirror. He then departed. With a smile on her face, Kilia watched *her ipo ahi*, her ardent lover, depart.

That night, a very angry uncle called Kilia to him, for the attendants had told him, when he returned, everything —how Kilia had eaten from the same calabash with the handsome young stranger, how she had laughed with him as he hovered over her breasts, how he had wrapped the silk around her waist. The uncle became wrathful when Kilia imperturbably told him she would marry the young man, for, like Ebenezer, hadn't she always had her own way?

"I shall be happy," she simply stated.

"Is happiness to be chosen before duty?" her uncle asked.

Kilia reflected. Hadn't her lover explained how the old ways were gone? Hadn't he convinced her that happiness mattered above all?

"Yes," she replied, "I choose happiness."

"A vow cannot be broken," her uncle reminded her. "The gods shall surely mete out great punishment for a broken vow. Who knows what terrible things shall happen?"

But Kilia was adamant; she would marry the young stranger.

When the chief to whom Kilia was betrothed heard this news, this breaking of the ʻolelo paʻa, this breaking of the vow, his eyes became cold with fury. In the old days, the handsome young stranger would be hunted down and killed. Kilia too would die by his own hand. But in these days, the mana of the white men was greater. The chief was powerless before the mana of the John Palmer Parker family, and he knew it. He had only one recourse, and that was secret revenge.

He asked to see Kilia one last time. Grabbing her violently, he jerked out a clump of her hair. He then brutally pushed her from him.

"You shall find out the meaning of breaking a vow," he said. "*E malama o loaʻa i ka niho*." "Be careful, or you will be caught in the teeth." He looked at her menacingly, and departed.

Though Kilia was shaken, having never experienced violence to herself before, she was pleased that the worse was over. Now she could begin preparations to sail across the sea to her love.

The jilted chief, however, made a night visit to the *kahuna ʻana ʻana*, the sorcerer of black magic. To him he gave the *maunu*, the bait—the black hair of Kilia. But this was not enough for the strong magic that the sorcerer must work. Under the guise of friendship, the sorcerer sent a woman, a wahine, to eat with Kilia. This wahine, when Kilia turned her back, scraped with a bit of coconut shell a bit of food from the calabash of Kilia, the same calabash from which the stranger had eaten.

69

Before Kilia departed, it was whispered to her that a great curse had been put upon her. Her attendants begged her not to go, but she was determined. Her love was greater than her fear.

Across the Channel, day after day Ebenezer saddled his horse, rode over the hills of Waimea, and stood in the morning winds, watching toward the island of Maui. Sick with love, he began to despair, and the meat began to drop from his bones.

Kipikane worried for him. Ebenezer had told his parents of his love for Kilia; John Palmer Parker was pleased that his son had found a woman he wished to wed, for it pleased him to envision a God-fearing dynasty living together for generations on a great expanse of land. Kipikane was very pleased that Ebenezer had chosen an ali'i chiefess, royalty like herself, but when she heard of the breaking of the vow, the 'olelo pa'a, she was troubled. She tried to explain to her son the sacredness with which her people held a promise; she related stories of broken promises, and black magic, and retaliation and death.

"But," said Ebenezer, looking at his mother with his winning smile, "*'I'ini o ka na'au*. She is my heart's desire."

Of the broken vow, the father, John Palmer said, with a dismissing wave of his hand, "These were the old ways. The old ways are gone. Children should not be betrothed at birth. It is heathenish. There is no black magic. Nothing shall come of this so-called broken vow."

At last, one beautiful spring morning, far in the distance, far out on the beautiful blue waters, on a *kai wahine*, a calm sea gentle like a woman, Ebenezer spied a flotilla of canoes. He waited and watched with expectant heart. Was that something white waving in the wind?

It was, and he excitedly took from his saddlebags his half of the white silk and this he waved to his beloved.

Kilia and Ebenezer wed June 7, 1849.

The *ohana nui*, the extended Parker family, was happy. The Parker Ranch was expanding rapidly. The family prospered quickly. Thousands of acres of land were annexed. Peach orchards and a profitable dairy were added. All three Parker children lived on the ranch with their spouses. The family ate together, prayed together, haole style, and laughed together. They were blessed indeed.

The men often teased their Hawaiian wives about their Hawaiian ways, and the women teased the men as well.

"When will you cook for us?" the men would ask and they would laugh, for in old Hawaii, only the kane, the men, cooked food. Kipikane and Kilia both had brought with them male attendants who performed this duty in the outer cookhouse, and this custom had not changed, even with the breaking of the kapus.

The women would laugh and pretend to be offended. "When you wear the *pa'u*, the skirt, we shall wear the malo, the loincloth," they would say and laugh.

The ardent love, the fire of love between Kilia and Ebenezer never abated, as it so often does after the first flames of passion between a man and woman. Kilia and Ebenezer had *ke aloha pili pa'a o ke kane me ka wahine*, the lasting love of man and woman, but for them every day was like the first day together, full of laughter, passion, and excitement. If Ebenezer were absent but a few hours, Kilia ran to him when he returned as if he had been gone for weeks. And Ebenezer always looked with longing at Kilia as if he were seeing her for the first time.

Joy and laughter were the seal of their relationship. They would sit and laugh together for many hours when Ebenezer tried to teach Kilia English. Ebenezer lavished expensive gifts on Kilia, especially when he returned from business trips to Oahu, trips he dreaded, as they took him away from his love. He returned laden with the finery of the white woman—dresses of silk, lace petticoats, high-heeled boots, great hats with plumed feathers. Kilia like best the feathers, as feathers were highly prized by the ancient Hawaiians. She would pluck the feather from the hat, and wear it around her neck, or in her hair. One night, to make him laugh, she surprised Ebenezer by wearing the high-heeled boots in bed! The bone corset made them both laugh and laugh, as she wore it lightheartedly underneath her pa'u. The truth was, she was not at ease in these strange clothes.

"You haole," she laughed, for she called him "you haole" though he was one-half Hawaiian. "*Haole ki ko'lea*," said Kilia, as she fingered the spiny stays of the corset, and smiled at Ebenezer.

"What does that mean?" asked Ebenezer.

"It means," she said, "you haoles are strange. For you see, my people will spend many hours and make great effort to catch the *ko'lea* bird. We will place a little bait with a bone attached to a string on a rock, and when the ko'lea eats the bait, the bone will lodge in its throat; thus, the bird is caught. You haoles, however, with your guns will blow a hole through the bird. Thus the bird is covered with his blood, what little is left of him. Very strange, you haoles. Haole ki ko'lea."

"You must show me sometime how to catch a ko'lea," teased Ebenezer, and he pulled her pa'u from her, for though it was true that he preferred to see her in her graceful and simple native dress, barefoot with her hair loose upon her shoulders, to the pretentiousness of the haole's dress, he most of all preferred to see her naked.

Only once did Ebenezer ask Kilia if she were happy; he had no need to ask her, he knew in his heart she was, for they could read one another's hearts—they shared one heart, as they shared all things.

"Do I look *hau'oli na maka*, do I look happy-eyed?" she asked him.

"You could have married a great chief," he reminded her.

"It was not meant to be," she replied, and she touched her nose to his. And it was true; she never thought of Maui, of Hana, or of her old life with longing.

"And what of that sorcerer?" asked Ebenezer. "Have you never feared him?"

"Never," said Kilia, and she tossed her long black hair defiantly, so that Ebenezer laughed.

Yes, they had shared everything. And as a symbol of their love, they always ate together from the same calabash. They shared laughter, their thoughts, they rode together on horseback, but there was one thing Kilia had never shared with Ebenezer—she had never shared that dream, that ho'ike na ka po from the 'aumakua that she had dreamed three days before seeing Ebenezer for the first time. Sometimes, but not often, she thought of it— the dream that revealed, "things shall not be as they were meant to be." She did not wish to tell Ebenezer what the wehewehe moe 'uhane had predicted—"You shall have great happiness, above all riches, but also, you shall suffer great sorrow, beyond all bearing."

Great happiness was surely hers. One after another, little babies were born. And Ebenezer stood by his wife, his true love, to share the moment of birth.

Happiness was surely hers, for she had everything—a loving husband, beautiful children, riches, pedigree.

One day Kilia playfully decided to show Ebenezer the Hawaiian way to catch a ko'lea bird. She waited patiently for hours until at last she caught the bird on a string. When she proudly showed the bird to Ebenezer, he laughingly dared her to cook it as well. This Kilia did.

Ebenezer ate one mouthful of the ko'lea bird. "This is quite good, Kilia. I think that from now on, you should always cook my dinner." He laughed, and Kilia laughed too. Ebenezer took another bite, and then another, but on the third bite, he choked.

Some little bone of the ko'lea bird was lodged in his throat. Ebenezer choked until he couldn't breathe, his face became purple, and he was on the brink of unconsciousness, when, with a great last effort, he thrust his back against the door again and again, until the bone dislodged from his throat. He swallowed hard, the bone passed down, and he could breathe again.

All this time Kilia was beside herself. Now she threw her arms around Ebenezer and sobbed to think that she had almost caused his death by choking. She was concerned about where the bone had gone, but Ebenezer said he felt fine.

In a matter of days, however, Ebenezer was dead. The bone had apparently lodged in his stomach, and he died of peritonitis.

Mad with grief, Kilia tore her hair, her clothes. When Ebenezer was laid in the ground, it was said Kilia became *kai hehene*, wild like the raging sea.

Kilia took her people, the servants who had been with her for a lifetime, and fled to the hills overlooking the ranch. She took her calabash too, and forbade her servants to clean it. Days and then weeks passed, and when John Palmer Parker looked up at the fires burning in the night, and listened to the drums, he questioned his wife Kipakane.

"This is the old way," said Kipikane. "The old way of grieving."

At last, John Palmer Parker said it was enough, for he was a practical man. Kilia must return, he said. Grief would pass. She must return to her children, to her duties as a mother. He sent for and had her brought home.

It was not the same Kilia that returned. The sorrowful, red-eyed, fragile woman with the unkempt hair resembled little the beautiful and radiant young woman who once had been known as Kilia. All who saw her were shocked at the extent of her transformation. For Kilia had no more interest in life.

The year of Ebenezer's death was 1855, and tragedy struck all around. In that same year, a great drought came upon the land of Waimea. Crops withered, blackened and shriveled up; the cattle began to die of thirst. John Palmer Parker had many worries, and one was for his despondent daughter-in-law and his grandchildren. Without consulting Kilia, and always practical, he chose a new husband for Kilia, a trusted man, a god-fearing man, who could become a member of the Parker ohana, take on the duties which had been Ebenezer's, and be a father to Kilia's children.

Kilia made little resistance to this plan, for in truth, for her, life was over. She thought often now of that dream she had had years ago. "This dream means two things: you shall have great happiness, above all riches, but it also means you shall suffer great sorrow, beyond all bearing." And she remembered well, "The happiness shall come first. And then the sorrow." So now was the time of sorrow.

The man chosen by John Palmer Parker to be Kilia's husband was a good man, a dutiful man, but in truth, after initial attempts to win her love, he gave up. He devoted all his interest to the Ranch. And Kilia? Even though she gave him one child, her heart was completely closed. Sad and morose, she kept to herself, and gave up the care of her children to the ohana and the servants. She was often found at Ebenezer's grave, sitting quietly, with vacant eyes.

In 1860, Kilia's son Ebenezer, just ten years old, died. In that same year, Rachel Keliikipakaneokaolohaka also passed.

In 1861, six years after the death of Ebenezer, Kilia gathered her servants together, for, for the first time since leaving Hana, she felt the wish to return to her childhood home. Her husband tried to discourage her, and John Palmer Parker forbade her to take the children; still, she would go.

In the same canoes in which she and her people had disembarked in Waimea on a beautiful, fair spring day in 1849, on a kai wahine, a calm sea gentle like a woman, she and her people departed for Hana. But this was not such a sea, not a sea like a gentle woman.

The day of departure was dark and cold, for a great storm was gathering force. The servants fearfully tried to dissuade Kilia, but she could not be dissuaded from departing. With trepidation, they cast off. Kilia turned and looked back toward Waimea. She saw again, standing on the hillside, her love, her Ebenezer, waving a white piece of silk.

Yes, she had had great happiness, more than the greatest riches. And now she suffered, more than she could bear. Tears flowed from her eyes like rain.

The sky darkened more and more, great thunderclaps rolled, and lightening bolts flashed all around. Great waves pounded over the canoes, and the servants were terrified. They could see the fish of the depths churning in the frothing, roiling waters that broke high above them. The woman servants screamed and the men servants rowed for their lives, but Kilia sat still and silent in the midst of kai hehene, the raging sea, looking back toward Waimea, until the tip of a great breaker hovered over them for a moment, like the frozen finger of death, then tilted and burst with fury over them, scattering their broken bones and carrying them away in the foaming sea.

****

WARRIOR WOMAN

She was a fierce as any warrior, and she knew it. She had told her man, the chief of her people, the last time she had lain with her cheek against his, *na 'uha 'olina*, their thighs rejoicing, that she was not afraid to die. And, she was not, but secretly, in her heart of hearts, she knew she could not, not now—the gods of all her ancestors, her gods, would protect her, and when she did die, she would do so many years from now, when her hair had grown white like the mist and her flesh was crinkled as a breadfruit and her bones would no longer carry her. Yes, it would be many years before she would leave her body from its bed of straw, drifting away from her corpse like a wisp of smoke, while her children's children and their children wailed all around her, tearing their hair and lamenting her going, perhaps even knocking out their teeth, for, after all, she was ali'i, a high chiefess. This vision of herself, far off into the future, pleased her, and she smiled. *E make auane'I loko o ku'u punana*—I shall die within my nest, she mused with satisfaction.

Her *waimaka lehua*, red water drops from the *'ohia lehua* tree, had stopped flowing, and she took this as an omen that all would be well, that she, her man, her children, her people would be protected; this was her last day in the *Hale Pe'a*, the menstrual house, for the kapu of the place of dark night would have made her unclean for tomorrow's coming battle.

Though she was reclining comfortably on her mat, she now gritted her strong white teeth when she thought of tomorrow's battle. She saw herself and her man and her man's warriors grinding the enemy into dust, dashing their bones into the rocks in fury. What they did later with those bones would give her great satisfaction—those bones would not be laid away in beautiful and valuable tapa cloths in caves, honored by their descendants for all time; they would not even be hidden in cairns beneath the black lava rocks—no, they would be used for fishhooks, or, and she smiled to think of it, their skulls would be used for excrement.

Her blood ran hot now when she thought of those cowards who would abandon the gods and the old ways, the sacred kapus. Her graceful brown hands clenched into ugly fists. What! Had the gods not given them everything, since the beginning of when time began—the luxuriant lands floating in the endless blue waters, across which the gods had led the ancestors safely, through many nights of starlight? Was it not the gods who gave them the good things to eat—the coconut and the rippling waters to drink? Was it not the gods who made the rain to fall and the taro to grow thick and lush? Was it not the heartbeat of the gods themselves in the very rhythm of the drums and the dance of the people's feet? Were they not surrounded by the gods—in every stone, in every tree, in every bird and fish? Was it not even a god who whistled in the pueo's call, the night bird god that led one safely out of the dark ominous forest and who was her own family 'aumakua? And was it not the gods who decided all fates —who should perish in the furious storms of the sea and who should die comfortable in their hales, attended all around by their loved ones?

Now those enemies of the aina, the enemies of the very land, were pulling down the heiaus, the temples to the gods. Men and women were breaking the most sacred of kapus and eating together in the same hale. Women were eating forbidden food that only men should eat. Her heart beat fast and she could rend apart those who were now saying...

She frowned and relaxed her hands while trying to understand. What were they saying? But she remained perplexed. Were they saying the gods were dead? But even a child knew the gods could not die. Were they saying the gods had lost their power? But if that were so, the sun would stop shining, the taro would shrivel and die, and the rains would not fall. Babies would fall shriveled and black and dead from their mother's wombs. This could not be! The power of the gods was forever! Her loyalty to the gods was forever! She snarled, just as she would do in battle on the day after this day. They would find out about the gods' power!

Inspired by her indignation, she suddenly stood to her feet and prepared to walk to the sea to purify herself. She was tall, as tall as her man, and well formed; indeed, childbirth had transformed the slim straight body of a girl, which had been willowy like water grass, into a body strong like earth, full of vitality, life, ardor.

As she strode the path to the sea, the prayer drums, the *pahu*, began to sound again and her own heart beat stronger. She stood in the hot afternoon sun at the water's edge and squinted up into the ball of white fire. What fools, she thought with anger, to disobey the gods.

She dove into the waves, and when she emerged, her long black hair spread about her face like a lei of black seaweed. *Keiki* were playing and laughing in the sand, and she watched them with intense interest. Yes, she thought, her children and her people's children would be safe— tomorrow and the next day and the next day they would play and laugh by the sea, protected by the gods, for her people obeyed the will of the gods. But the enemy's children?

She saw into the future—she saw them hungry, thirsty, crying, with no one to bring them nourishment—*keiki makua'ole*—children without parents. They would perish in the fiery sun or alone in the dark night, their fathers and mothers never returning. In spite of her anger and indignation and resolution, pity touched her heart to think of the suffering children, for, after the gods, her people loved children beyond all things. And were not the enemies and her people *pili ma ka hanauna*, all having a common ancestor, all sharing the same *piko*, the same umbilical cord?

She waded from the water and sat on a hot rock, combing her fingers through her long black hair, listening to the intensifying sound of the pahu. The men would be making their final preparations, honing their knives and spears, tightening the shark teeth on the weapon that would slice a man's genitals in half in one stroke, practicing the slingshot, which with good aim and help from the gods could burst a man's head open with a single blow.

She heard a great shout by the men go up, and she knew Ku the Red-Feathered, the great god of war, horrible with his shark's teeth grimace and vacant eyes of pearly shell, was being carried on his stick among the warriors, inciting them to bloodlust and fury. She thought with pride of her own man, for he was the chief of all chiefs to whom had been entrusted Ku the war god when the late great king had passed. It was her man's duty, and honor, to protect the terrible Red-Feathered god.

This would be a great battle; some would not return. She wondered, almost idly, who would not return, which cousins and uncles and brothers would leave their women to wail and lament in the night. True, her own husband might not return—she could not know his destiny, only her own, for the gods would speak to her only of her own destiny, not that of others, even her man. She would make her offering this evening of ti leaves for the safety of her man, and also that he might be very brave, and that he might kill many of the enemy. She had no doubt of this, for above all the chiefs, her man was skilled in *lua*, the arts of war.

It was said throughout the islands that her man had been given by the war god Ku himself, the gift of *aalolo*, by which he could strike a man so swiftly and deftly as to cause paralysis and then, by the Ku-given gift of *hakihaki*, break every bone in the enemy's body, beginning with the little finger of the hand and ending with snapping the back. She pictured with satisfaction her man carrying the bundle of broken bones, still alive, back to the altar to be sacrificed to the bloodthirsty Red-Feathered one. Her man was especially skilled too with the *piki 'ikoi*, the tripping weapon, after which, once he caused the enemy to fall, he finished him with the *ka'ane*, the strangulation cord.

Of course, the enemy too had great warriors, *koa kane* who were also adept in the various war skills. The enemy too had a bone breaker and those who were deft with the strangulation cord, but what the enemy did not have was Ku, the Red-Feathered One. And it was true; no man excelled her man in the arts of war.

Tenderness swept over her heart when she thought of her husband. She remembered now how they lain together five nights ago, their thighs rejoicing. She had searched his face with her fingers, while he had lain so still in the dark beneath her. Why was he so quiet, she had wondered? He had seemed preoccupied with thoughts that she could not divine.

At last, she had whispered, "What are you thinking?"

For a long time, he had been silent. Then he had said, "Three nights ago I dreamed I carried a calabash of water, and I stumbled, and the calabash broke, and the water flowed over the sands."

81

She had lain silent, reflecting, for everyone knew that the dream of a broken calabash and spilt water foretold death.

"And two nights ago," her man had continued, "I dreamed of an empty canoe, sailing upon dark waters."

"A loved one shall die?" she had whispered, for all knew that the dream of a canoe upon dark waters betokened death.

"And last night," her man had said, "I dreamed of a knife in my piko."

She had remained silent, thinking of this, for everyone knew that a dream of injury to one's piko, one's navel, one's link to all one's kin and to the ancestors, foretold death.

"I am thinking too," he had said, "it is strange that that the red feathers of Ku have not bristled. I am thinking this is not a good sign. The kahu too, the keeper of Ku the Red-Feathered, is worried. Always before, when a battle will be victorious, the feathers of Ku have bristled and stood on end."

She had pondered this for some time. Being a woman, she had never seen the awful and terrifying Ku, his feathers standing upright with the mana of blood thirst, being carried about on a stick by the kahuna, as the men roared and the drums beat furiously, inciting the men to bloodletting.

"How could Ku the Red-Feathered not be with us?" she had asked aloud. "We go in his defense, and in defense of all the gods. Surely victory will easily be ours."

"The enemy has the rolling gun of the white man which we do not have," her man had simply replied. "Many will die."

"They are cowards to hide behind the rolling gun," she had said contemptuously, for everyone knew that the measure of a warrior and his courage was his skill to fight face to face. "A man must fight eyeball to eyeball."

"Yes," he had said, "a man should fight eyeball to eyeball. But since the haoles have come …men are no longer men. Men hide behind the long guns and the rolling gun."

"Yes, many may die," she had repeated softly. "But the gods will be with us. We shall roast the dead in *imus* like black pigs. We shall scoop out their eyeballs. We shall flay their skin from their bodies while they yet live."

They had lain still for a long time, but her heart was beating loudly. "*Auwe*," "O," she said, not so much to her man as to the spirits of the dark night, "but to be a man, to dance in the midst of battle, to kill with my bare hands…" for the blood of her own great ancestor, a woman warrior, a koa wahine, ran in her veins. And her own man had secretly taught her some of the skills of the koa kane, how to hold and thrust a spear where a man was most vulnerable to the dagger. She lay thinking of these things.

Then her man had said softly, "You must obey very carefully what I tell you. You must do exactly what I say."

She had laughed softly, and he had laughed too, for they both knew she was very obstinate, and did as she pleased.

"Now listen," he had continued, "you must stay far behind the fighting men, with the women. You must carry the gourds with water and food, but you must not come into the fight. No matter what happens, no matter how the blood should flow, you must return safely to the keiki and old ones."

"I will be near you, wherever you are," she had said determinedly, and she had stroked his cheek lovingly.

"But I am forbidding you," he had said.

"Yes," she had laughed, "you are forbidding me. Still, I will be near you."

He had sighed, for he knew she was brave, resolute, and willful. Finally, to ease his heart, she had promised to stay behind the fighting men, if only she could be in sight of him at all times.

"If you will remain behind the fighting, I will make you then a little bird's nest, made of baby ferns and sweet moss, hidden in the sweet-smelling pili grasses, where you may watch in safety," her man said teasingly, and he had laughed and stroked her hair.

"Yes, a little bird's nest," she replied, and she had laughed with him, "and in between slaughtering the enemy you will come and rest with this mama bird and she will enfold you in her wings and we will snuggle close. Like this."

And she had wrapped him tight against her warm breasts and pressed her pelvis into his. They had both laughed, and once more, their thighs had rejoiced, and finally they had fallen asleep in one another's arms, her breath warm on his shoulder.

Now, sitting on a rock looking out to the endless sea, intense love, *kipona aloha*, like the warm sunshine, flowed over her and melted her heart when she thought of her man, her chief. No man was braver, no man was stronger, no man more skillful in the war-games than her man. She knew all would be well. The gods were with them.

She wrapped herself in her kapa and walked thoughtfully back to the woman's hale, thinking of all the preparations still to be done before the nighttime. Many coconuts must be stored in the canoes, for tomorrow would be a thirsty day. She must give instructions to the old ones for the care of the children, but most importantly of all, she must make her ti-leaf offering to the gods.

Can it be, she thought, and she stopped for a moment with the shock of the thought, that the enemy will make no offering to the gods? But if they no longer obey the gods, they will not make offerings. And if they do not make offerings, how could they be victorious?

She snorted contemptuously, and her step became lighter. All would be well. The temples the enemy had ordered thrown down would be erected again, stone by stone, and honor and order would be re-established in the land. The kapus would be obeyed, the ali'i would rule, and the commoners would obey. Men would eat only with men, and women would eat only with women. The gods were with those who honored them; the gods protected those who fed them the black pig in the family temple, and sacrificed the bloody pig with two legs in the war heiaus.

Not until late, late in the night did she finally sleep. The pahu had beat furiously, the black pig had been offered, and the men had shouted until her blood too had boiled, like theirs, into an animal frenzy, but at last the sound of the pahu had faded away into the ultimate solemnity of sacred silence, and the shadows of the night had dissolved into darkness and oblivion. Total stillness ruled the night, and it was only the *kapuna*, the very old, who lay awake, pondering the morrow, worrying, and then offering their worry and fear up to the gods. The children slept as do all children, with no fear of tomorrow, peacefully. The others, the women and the warriors, especially the warriors, had withdrawn their souls deep into their bodies, gathering mana, divine power; for tomorrow's glory, they must be rested.

Before the stars began to fade, she had a ho'iki na ka po, a revelation of the night. In her dream, she was a she-bird nestling with her chicks in the grass, one chick under each wing, when a terrible roar caused her to start, and before she could hold her chicks tight, a huge wave engulfed everything, and her nest and her chicks were scattered in dark waters.

*

She opened her eyes from which tears fell like rain, and for a moment did not know where she was, until she heard the sounds of others outside the hale stirring. Then she remembered. This was the day of battle. There was no time to think of the meaning of the dream, or tell it to a wehewehe moe 'uhane, a dream interpreter. She bound from her mat and went to the sleeping children. She silently watched them for a moment, then bent and placed her cheek next to theirs. A wizened old woman crouched beside them, watching. Their eyes met; the old one's eyes were empty but her own eyes blazed with fire. She tightened her kapa and then hurried from the hale, down the path to the canoes. A great bold moon lit the way.

Only a murmur of the deep voices of men stirred over the water. The women who were going were quiet. All knew their places and the canoes drifted away silently from the dark shore. They rode their canoes quietly and stealthily on the waves like narrow-eyed man-eating sharks through the night, led by the great moon and the last of the stars. She carried in her lap the sacred yellow-feathered cape and the terrifying gourd helmet her man, her chief, would wear in battle. Ku the Red-Feathered god was carried in the first canoe, imbibing mana. They all felt it, with every dipping of an oar into the water—Ku was very angry, and hungry.

In the first light of morning, she was amazed to see that hundreds of canoes floated about her in all directions. Warriors from every district in the land, loyal to the gods and the old ways, had heeded the summons of her man, the chief. Never had she seen so many warriors gathered together. Men began to shout boastfully from one canoe to another, and there was even the sound of men laughing. The faces of the men were hideous, tattooed with spots and dots or their whole faces solid black.

Ku the Red-Feathered was delighted.

Her man's canoe was, after the canoe that carried Ku the war god, the first to round the bay of battle, and the flotilla of canoes and men became silent. Sunlight was just squinting over the tops of the hills and the night's chill was still in the air. Dolphins danced and leaped about the canoes, greeting the new day with joy and causing her to laugh quietly to herself. Through the green water illuminated by the golden sun, she could see rainbow-colored fishes darting from the shadows of the canoes. A great school of iridescent needlefish stood like silent sentinels as her canoe skimmed past. She became mesmerized by the silver wavelets which danced about her hand as she trailed it in the water and she felt childlike again, happy and free.

Was it not such things that made one truly happy? Silver waves and great white moons and the golden light of the sun? Sea breezes kissing one's face, salt spray on one's lips, the sound of lapping water? A whole beautiful day before one, to do as one chose? To play as the dolphins play? Yes, she felt light and happy.

Suddenly she felt the canoe put into the sand with a jolt, and her reverie ended. A great swell of voices sounded like thunder, and many conch shells began to blow menacingly as the men sprang from the canoes. She saw in one glance that the hales of the people on the beach and hillside were empty; she knew the old ones and children and women had sought refuge in the hills beyond.

Well they might, she thought casually, for the blood of their men shall fill the waters.

She shaded her hands against the glare of the sun and looked into the far distance. There they were, the line of enemy, those who would dare to disobey the gods, those who had toppled the houses of the gods. They stood like grey tiki in the distance, without moving. Watching.

For the sake of the gods, she hated them.

The men now were rubbing oil onto their bodies, so that in the morning light they looked like fish just pulled from the waters; except for the chiefs, in the great-feathered cloaks, they would go into battle oiled and naked. For how could an enemy hold a slippery fish? The muscles in their necks and legs and arms shown so bright and grew so big that she dared not look longer at this world of the man, the kane, preparing to fight hand to hand, preparing to kill, and she lowered her eyes while silently helping the other women to unload the provisions of food and water.

So, she thought, it must be like this when women give birth— kane must feel humble at the world of wahine, men must look away from a world they cannot ever enter. We are all warriors in this world, she thought. What matters is that we are brave warriors, men and woman. What matters is that we are fearless in the face of death. Men and women.

When she did look up again, it was as though the men had disappeared, and in their places were strange and frightening beings with huge heads of wood upon which red and yellow feathers waved menacingly, with white eyes deep in black sockets.

These had arranged themselves in various companies behind their chiefs. A great phalanx of near-impenetrable warriors armed with *pololus,* javelins that would rip out the entrails of the enemy, was flanked by those carrying *pahoas*, daggers as sharp as razors, for tearing out the eyeballs, and those carrying *lei-o-mano*, the shark-tooth weapon. Others carried long war clubs that would split a man's head in two with one stroke, and many carried slingshots and the dreadful throwing ax. Behind them were the commoner warriors, the oiled ones, armed with stone hand clubs and sticks like razors. In the center of this fearsome assembly, protected by the *a'olohe*, the expert bodyguards, was her man. Her heart thrilled with pride to see him in his yellow-feathered cape, his weapons of death tucked into his malo.

Suddenly the *kahuna ki'i*, the priest carrying Ku into battle ahead of the chief, screamed a terrifying and bloodcurdling shriek, the conch shells blew piercingly, and the great formation of many hundreds advanced toward the enemy. Yet the enemy stood quiet and still. This should have been an omen, but it was not heeded. She picked up her calabashes of water, and motioned to the other women to follow the men at a distance.

Across the sand they marched, the women far behind the warriors, until the men stopped a long javelin's throw from the enemy. It was the custom through all the ages that a challenger from each side should step forward and hurl insults at the other, inciting one another to battle. This was the *oli ho'oulu*, the taunting chant. From her people's side, a great hulk of a warrior advanced, and all were silent. Waving a heavy war club in the air, then striking the ground like thunder, he shouted epithets that no man should hear without his blood boiling.

"Dogs," he shouted, "eaters of filth!"

Strangely, no contender stepped forward from the enemy. Still the enemy stood like silent tikis. She herself moved closer behind the men, in order to see more clearly. The challenger shouted more insults, and turned to his warriors with bloodshot enraged eyes, and he laughed loudly and obscenely.

"Eaters of filth!" he shouted, "we shall cook you cowards and feed your sour flesh to the pigs," and he made an obscene gesture, and all the men of her people laughed with him.

Suddenly, there was a great sound like a thunderbolt, and dust and rocks and sand filled the air. As the dust cleared, she saw men running in every direction, and many lay on the ground, screaming, though some lay unmoving. An empty helmet with black sockets rolled near her feet. The women behind her shrieked with terror and fled back toward the water. She searched with earnest eyes through the dust for the yellow-feathered cape.

She spied it in the heat and fury and discerned that the phalanx that had broken was struggling to form again. She saw her man turn toward his warriors and lift one arm of the feathered cape out to his side, so that it shone in its magnificence like a magnificent yellow bird with golden wing outstretched in the wind. He raised his other arm in a gesture of command to advance forward and she thrilled with pride at the sight. Now the cowards will taste blood, she thought.

At that very moment, the great rolling gun thundered again, accompanied by a hail of bullets from the long guns which spit everywhere into the air around them, and the dust and rocks and sand were blinding. It seemed as though everyone, men and women, were screaming and running. She herself was knocked to the ground in the chaos, so that blood ran from a rock wound in her leg. She stood up and tried to see through the chaos.

Where was her man? Where was the yellow-feathered cloak? She ran forward through men who were fleeing backward. More long guns were spitting death. Men were falling to the ground all around her. The sickly smell of blood began to waft into the air.

In disbelief, she saw the great yellow cloak lying on the ground in the distance, like a great yellow bird fallen from the sky and broken in the dust. Now she saw the enemy, many hundreds, rushing toward her people, smiting the fallen with stones and daggers, spears and clubs.

"My people, onward!" she screamed.

A warrior lay motionless on the ground. She stooped to his side for his spear and saw with shock that the face that had once been her man's brother was blown away. She gathered the spear and ran forward, screaming, exhorting her people not to flee, to advance forward.

As she neared the yellow-feathered cloak, she saw with astonishment the Red-Feathered god Ku-ka-ili-moku lying on the ground. Trampled by many feet, the stick he rode was broken in the dust, one eye was missing, his feathers were broken and bits of red were scattered in the sand and blowing in the wind. A fleeing man, without seeing, mashed the face of Ku into the ground with his foot. She stood for a moment and looked at the misshapen remnants of Ku with amazed horror.

Her man too was lying with his face in the ground. She dropped the spear to her side and with difficulty she turned him on his back. Red sticky blood poured from a great hole in his chest. Kneeling, she called to him. He opened his eyes.

"You have left the sweet nest in the grass I have made for you," he said with difficulty.

"Yes, I have left my sweet nest in the grass," she replied tenderly.

"You are a stubborn woman," he said.

"Yes, I am a stubborn woman," she replied very softly.

He smiled, and closed his eyes.

She spread the great beautiful feather cloak gently over him, to hide the ugly red wound. She looked up and saw the enemy coming toward her, one with a long gun, the other making the gestures of the bone breaker. The bone breaker made an obscene gesture and smirked. She grabbed the spear and stood to her feet.

"Auwe, cowards!" she cried. "You shall not break the bones of my man."

Still the two advanced toward her, the long gun, and the bone breaker.

She raised the spear with both arms and with her whole soul made ready to thrust it into the bone breaker, but laughing outright, the one with the long gun raised his arm and fired into her face.

The spear which she held fell from her hands, blood poured from her temple, and she sank down slowly, so slowly, upon her man, her chief, as if she were snuggling down to dream an eternal dream of love, upon a downy nest of golden sacred feathers.

WHERE HAS HE GONE?

She had seen horror many times; it had never disturbed her, she was accustomed to it. She had watched her father kill men right before her eyes when she was but a young child, and it had affected her no more than watching a dog or a pig slaughtered. She had seen pigs trussed and men trussed and carried into the sacrificial heiaus many times, but such events were merely commonplace and necessary incidents in the rhythm of her days. She had seen men, and women, butcher one another on battlefields; she had seen blood flow like water from deeds of violence, but rather than tremble at such dreadfulness, she had felt proud, for her people had always fought heroically, and heroism is what most mattered. But now as she restlessly paced the beach below the heiau, and heard the low, monotonous rhythm of the death drums coming from the hale koko, the blood house, she shuddered.

It was *haipo*, a night sacrifice. She whispered a command for her attendants to go away, which they did instantly and silently, with great trepidation, for to make even the slightest sound, even the crunch of a footfall on sand, while a man was being offered to the gods, would be instant death. When they had departed, and she was alone, she stopped pacing and looked up in desperation at the heavens, but all was black; not a single star shone. She turned and looked toward the sea for solace—her beloved sea—but even the ancient waters were dark and silent, the comforting primeval sound of the waves lost in the beat of the drums. Surely, the gods were brooding.

She sat down cross-legged on the sand, with her back toward the sea, enveloped by the elemental darkness and the primordial sound of the drums. Every few moments she would look up at the heiau—but in the blackness of the night, she could see nothing but the torches burning. She knew, however, what was happening inside the heiau. Remorse, for the first time in her life, flooded her haughty heart, for, upon the *lele*, the sacrificial altar, lay her young lover, only nineteen years old.

She was said, by all the explorers from distant lands who had touched upon these islands, as well as by her own people, to be the most beautiful woman in Polynesia. And the most formidable. She was the daughter of one of the fiercest warriors and highest chiefs of the land, and her mother was a great queen, by virtue of having been married to another high king. The blood that flowed through her veins, and the mana, the spirit power, linked her with the most royal blood of Maui. And she was the favorite queen of the king.

Six feet tall, vigorous and highly intelligent, fiercely independent, in the full beauty of her womanhood, she was a matchless consort for a matchless king. The king knew they were perfectly matched, she knew it, the people knew it. *Iwi kani*, the people said, when they spoke of their king and queen. Strong bones. Strength. Nevertheless, the queen might prove to be extremely dangerous, for so the omens had warned—of this, the king was advised by the *kahuna nui*, his high priest. And so it had been true, for more than one man had lost his life because of her.

It had been predicted by a great prophet that she would be loved by and marry a great king. And so she had. She had been married to the king when she was very young, some said only ten, some said thirteen; he had been more than twice her age. He had not been king then; he

94

had been a high chief already renowned for his valor as a warrior, his great strength, his cunning, and his self-reliance. He was called "The Lonely One," and his name fit, for he kept his own counsel. He had been impressed not only by her beauty and robustness, which was already strikingly evident at her young age, but by her boldness, which was equal to his own. She had stridden fearlessly up to him, after a battle in which her kinsmen had been slain, and demanded the body of a high chief, her cousin. He had been much amused by her audacity, but he had given her what she wanted. And then he had married her.

It was said that, in the beginning, she did not love him. Not only was he so much older, a grown man and she a lovely young girl, but his face was far from an attractive face—his brow was naturally heavily creased so that he always wore a look of ferocity and harshness. In fact, he was sometimes called "ax-face." She did, however, admire him. It was said that he had lifted the immense Pohaku Naha stone, and the prophecy ran that whoever could lift the stone would rise to power and become the ruler of all the islands. Being strong willed and obstinate, but also astute, she had finally consented to marry him on one condition—that her children by him would be the heirs to the kingdom. The king agreed. Indeed, he wanted her badly.

Her name meant "Great Thundering Bird Feather," and she was named for her maternal uncle, the Mo'i of Maui, who had gathered under his control all the islands from Maui to Ni'ihau. For the king to marry her was *'imi haku*, to marry one of higher rank than himself. Their children would be born of higher rank than himself, thus increasing mana, spirit power, not only for himself, and his descendants, but for his ancestors, for the gods, and, particularly and ultimately, for Wakea, the divine, progenitor power that had created the land, all sustenance, and the Ali'i Nu'i, the first man. And for the ali'i, the

95

chiefly caste, the ruling class, mana was the quest of life, the Holy Grail of life, for mana was the power that sustained *kanaka*, the entire race of human kind, the ali'i as well as the *maka'aina*, the commoners. Without mana, all creation would collapse.

And Wakea, God of gods, fed upon koko, blood.

There were two ways of attaining mana, and both were by blood sacrifice. One way was through violence, and the other, through sex.

By the killing and offering of the blood of victims to the gods, by feeding blood to the gods, the delighted Wakea in turn blessed one's ancestors, one's descendants, and oneself with mana. Successful warring and skills in killing were therefore greatly esteemed. Great chiefs were great conquerors, not great peacemakers. The search for mana was the reason for the never-ending warfare, more than other.

The other way Wakea fed was upon the blood of birthing women. A child, birthed upon the red amniotic flood of *'ina 'ina*, represented the sum totality of the genealogical strain. The great birthing stones, the tabooed *pohaku hanau*, upon which the ali'i wahine, the royal chiefesses, labored and groaned, surrounded in state by high chiefs who were witnesses to the birth of ali'i, were blood altars to Wakea. The purer the bloodline of the newborn—the more directly related to Ali'i Nui, the first man—the better the blood, the closer to God. Thus, mating with a woman of higher lineage lifted up the entire race.

For the first years of her marriage with the king, life was very happy for the young queen. Though the king had other wives, some said three, some said seven—eventually he would have more than 20 wives—it mattered not at all to her, for she was the most pleasing to him—of this she was certain. Being of such high royal lineage, she was given everything she wanted, and with her natural confidence and cleverness, she seized everything that she regarded as hers with royal prerogative, including the king's affections. And he willingly gave his affections, for he found her not only beautiful, sexually alluring, and entertaining, but he found something in her that was like him, something that assuaged and comforted his lonely self. They were kindred souls.

The young, beautiful, and headstrong queen was also flirtatious and enticed other high chiefs into her tempting arms, indifferent to the king's feelings on this matter, and indifferent to the fates of the unlucky high chiefs. Politically astute, the king, rather than challenging the illicit lover directly, and alienating factions that supported the offending chief, would wait for an opportune time and reason to have the lover slain. In this way, one high chief, said to be the most handsome man in all the islands, a great and fearless warrior, and a former ally to the king, was dispatched.

Nevertheless, but for one exception, the queen grew to love the king more than anyone and anything; that one exception was the sea, and she often told him so. This would make the king laugh, this subtle allusion to the queen's infidelity, for the king and queen never openly spoke of her transgressions; to do so would have been beneath the dignity of both.

"It is true," she would say, with a daring look as if she were confessing to faithlessness, "I love the sea more than you," and she would splash him with water as they played in the waves.

"I will kapu the sea," said the king, with mock anger, and he wrinkled his already-deeply furrowed brow with mock seriousness, "and forbid you two to come together, upon pain of death."

The queen would toss her head haughtily and respond, "Upon whose death, O king? For you could kill neither the sea nor me." And away she swam, racing a wave, with the king in pursuit.

Her prowess as a swimmer was known and admired throughout the islands, and she surfed the high waves as well as any man, and better than most. She could read the sea as well as any man too; she could name the wave that breaks diagonally, the receding wave, the rough wave, the wave that shoots high. She knew a day before when the sea would become *kai akua*, the gods' sea, a raging sea so dangerous that one could not survive it, and she knew a day before when the sea would become *kai wahine*, the woman sea, the gentle sea. She could read the currents; she always knew when the tide would rise and ebb, and she knew exactly when mid-tide would occur. She and the king were often seen frolicking in and riding the waves, and it was well known she had challenged him in the waters, and won. Never a day passed but she spent many hours in the sea, swimming great distances, which shaped her long, lean body with agility and grace.

There were other ways in which she challenged the king. When they were alone, they would debate matters that, by custom, only the *ali'i kane*, the high chiefs, might argue. Sometimes he might ask her opinion on important issues, even war matters, and he came to respect her advice as much as his chiefs' and his kahunas'. She also cajoled the king into revealing his innermost thoughts and plans, which none but his war god Ku knew. In this way, she became privy to his secret desire, and the mandate of his god, to conquer and rule the entire chain of islands.

Thus, for the first few years of her marriage, the world as she saw it revolved around herself. Then, two surprising events occurred which enlarged her perspective and were to have great significance for herself and her people.

The mighty ships of the foreigners sailed into the islands. The lusty haoles, the white sailors who had been

98

at sea for months, dangled trinkets—beads, mirrors, iron nails—before the covetous eyes of the island wahines, who swam naked by the hundreds to the ships, exchanging their favors for baubles and good times. The young queen watched them go, happy and laughing, and she watched them swim back to shore, happy and laughing, but, being an ali'i wahine, a chiefess of the royal class, she could not partake of these simple pleasures. It also reached her ears that the wahines were breaking the strictest kapu of all, punishable by death—the primordial prohibition that men and women could not eat together. The wahines were openly eating with the sailors, and not only that, they were enjoying forbidden food, food that was kapu to the women, including pork, bananas, coconuts.

When the queen first heard these shocking reports, she was sure the offenders, haoles and wahines, would be struck dead by the gods, but, when instead the wahines became merrier and merrier, and paraded about happily with their easily-won treasures, and the haoles seemed to be none the worse, but quite the more content, she began to wonder. She discussed this with the king, who was equally bewildered, but being a devout believer in his gods and their kapus, his final words on the subject were, "We shall see."

It was not the trinkets, the beads and mirrors and iron nails, that the queen began to resent, for, being the favorite queen, she could acquire these things by simply asking for them from the king, who could demand them from the haoles. But, being young, naturally playful, and passionate, it was the good times, the merriment, that she was missing out on, that irritated her. Why should she not eat the forbidden foods? Why should she not swim out to the ships and make love with one of these exotic white men? For the first time in her life, she questioned, though only to herself, the *kapu 'illi*, the many taboos inherited from the chiefly ancestors. Previously, she had taken these for granted. Was not all life governed by the kapus? Was not the breaking of the kapu a theft of mana? Did not the kapus protect, above all, the ali'i caste?

She watched as the sailors stood about laughing with derision and jostling one another, when her people, chiefs and commoners, fearfully seated themselves on the ground at once when the king's possessions, his food, or bath water were carried by. Was not this, the breaking of the *kapu noho*, punishable by death? Yet the sailors did not die, or seem to suffer ill effects from this sacrilege. She pondered these things carefully in her own mind, and watched.

The people, and especially the ali'i, began to acquire a taste for what the foreigners had to offer. The king wanted their weaponry and war knowledge, and traded his vast forests of sandalwood, and ultimately the lives of his people, for them; the queen, naturally competitive and fun loving, became an avid player of cards. She began to smoke a pipe. And, she developed a strong liking for *waikulu*, the water of fire, rum.

This fateful event, the arrival of the white foreigners, began to shake the foundations of untold centuries of entrenched cultural tradition—the religious and political structure of the islanders—and, the minds of the people. But on a more personal level, the mind of the queen was rocked by another event which was to awaken her to something within herself she didn't know existed—the fire of jealousy.

The king, as was customary for kings, had taken other wives, mostly for political reasons, as marriage was the primary means to cement political alliances. The queen, always confident that no one could supplant her in the king's affections, was not disturbed in the least by these marriages. Besides, none of these wives, though all chiefesses, possessed the pedigree that she possessed. But when some years had passed, and it became evident that the queen was barren, and that she could never give the king an heir to his kingdom, the king married the most highborn chiefess of the islands, an aristocrat of such pureblooded stature that even the king had to approach her on his knees. Besides being of almost godlike lineage, claiming royal descent from four chiefly lines, this girl was years younger than the queen, and the king liked young girls. Besides, she was very beautiful. By mating with this girl, the king's children would be semi-divine. And indeed, her name meant "The Gathering of the Clouds of Heaven." Such high mana was hers, she possessed the *kapu moe*, the prostrating kapu, which required all who came into her presence, including the king, to fall full length to the ground.

Moreover, in order to win this girl, the king had humbled himself before her dying grandmother, who was of the highest royal rank, and asked to marry her. The dying queen consented, and in token of his respect to the queen and in thankfulness to the gods, the king had knocked out two of his front teeth.

The queen burned with jealousy. However, she took great pains to conceal it, for it was the noble duty of the king, even the righteous duty of the king, to uplift the race by purifying the bloodlines of the ali'i. It would be ignoble for the queen to hinder by petty feelings this sacred duty; jealousy did not serve to safeguard the race. Instead, she kept her enemy close, and she sublimated her envy and competitive nature by bending the girl's will to her own, dominating her, for the girl was sweet and as pliable as a young tree branch. Indeed, this young girl—whose mana was so great that if her shadow were to fall upon one, that unfortunate one would instantly be put to death—this girl was so gentle and compassionate, that she took great care to go about only at night, so as never to cause harm to her people. For that, the people accorded her great love and respect.

The queen began to drink heavily, and though she still swam daily, she spent most of her days at cards. She took great satisfaction in commanding the other noble ladies to drink until they were intoxicated and acting foolish, and when the king was away, as he often was for days at a time, performing his religious duties at the temple—for he was a religious man—she conducted orgies of revelry and drunkenness. She began to eat taboo foods, not so secretly, and it began to be rumored that she was indiscriminate in love. However, even when inebriated, she was cunning and proud, and no one suspected the envy she hid in her heart. No one except the king. For she and the king were too much alike to hide their hearts from one another.

The king, understanding his queen's hidden humiliation, appointed her to the highest offices of his reign, giving her unheard of power as an ali'i wahine, and he appointed her as the foster mother of any children who should be his heirs. He honored her by making her lands and her self, *puuhonua*, places of refuge, so that she had the god-like power of life and death. Thus, she became admired and feared almost as much as the king, by ali'i and commoners alike.

Nevertheless, the queen's debauchery continued. And the rumors did not escape the king's ears.

The king forbade the orgies and put a kapu on the rum for everyone but himself—he allowed himself half a glass a day—but the queen disregarded the prohibition when the king was away, and continued as before. The king, unwilling to punish his favorite queen and humiliate her publicly, pretended therefore not to know of the drunken revelry.

But the thought of the queen's lovers tormented the king, and it began to be whispered about that he was mad with jealousy; however, it was more than jealousy that disturbed the king and made his mind uneasy and his

102

already-heavy brow furrow with dark premonition. For the queen knew all his secrets, his desires and his plans. She knew the conversations he had with Ku his war god. She knew the prayers he prayed in his war temple. It was at this point that his kahuna nui warned him of the omens.

"If ever one has the power to foment rebellion, it is your queen," whispered the kahuna nui.

The king, being by nature very reflective and farsighted, and a great strategist, considered the meaning of the omens carefully. The queen by birth was aligned with some of the most powerful clans in the islands. He himself had granted her unheard of powers of life and death. Her natural abilities, her sharp intellect and shrewdness, had attracted to her devoted supporters.

The king also weighed the truth that it was the most natural thing in the world that lovers confide their secrets to one another. What secrets might she divulge into the ear of some chief who lay on her mat, resting in her arms after a night of love? Yes, his queen could be very dangerous. At last, with a stroke of genius, and perhaps as a last resort, the king put a kapu on his queen!

"'*Eono moku a Kamehameha ua noa ia 'oukou, aka o ka hikao ka moku ua kapu ia na'u*," declared the king to all his people. "Six of my islands are free to you, but the seventh is kapu, and is for me alone."

The seventh island was the queen.

The queen, for her part, laughed, and was quite willing to ignore the kapu upon herself, and continue to take lovers when and if she wished. And she haughtily told the king so. For she had no fear of the king and his kapus. After all, she knew he could kill neither her nor the sea. But, with such a heavy penalty hanging over their heads, that of instant death, the pool of would-be lovers dried up, and no man dared to touch the queen.

*

The boy was handsome, tall and strong. He was intelligent, brave and skilled in the art of lua, the war games. He was the nephew of the king, and had been raised in court as a foster son. He was also proud and arrogant as young warriors who would become great warriors are. He was a favorite of the king, but one night, during a drunken orgy, with her liquid brown eyes, her swaying hips, the queen had invited the boy to sleep with her. He had come, like an immortal young god, to her hale and they had made love, their thighs rejoicing, until just before dawn, when he had departed, leaving her with a smile on her lips. But her servant, in fear of his own life if he did not tell, had already imparted the tryst to the king long before *alaula*, the flaming road of dawn, even while the heavens were yet burning with the night stars, even while the queen yet lay with her long legs entwined about her young lover. The king, without hesitation, ordered the boy's instant death.

*

He had come in the black of night to the boy's hale and stood in the shadows, awaiting his victim's return, the executioner with his strangulation cord. When, at dawn, the boy stooped to enter the doorway, the strangler stepped quickly forward, so that before the boy understood what was happening, the noose was around his neck, there was the sound of bone snapping, and his neck was broken. With another deft movement, the noose was tightened so that the boy would never draw another breath.

Thus, the body of the offering was perfectly unblemished, as it lay upon the lele, the sacrificial altar.

Now, sitting on the sand, alone on the beach, she remembered again how it was to lay with the boy. He had held her in his strong arms and loved her with the passion with which only the young can love. His passion had made her young again, for he had loved her all night long. He had whispered in her ear, with the innocence and ardor of the young lover, praises of her beauty, and his devotion, and he had held her close as if he would never let her go, as if never had he held such treasure. And she? She had surrendered herself and her body completely to his caresses. And when the stars had begun to fade, and he had reluctantly risen to go, the young lover fumbling in the dark for his loincloth, he had politely asked her permission to come again. And it was this that had made her smile as she had fallen to sleep, and it was this that had made her smile when she had awakened in the morning.

The sound of the drums ceased; now she could hear the haunting sound of the waves lapping very gently upon the shore. An eerie chanting, like an otherworldly moaning, began. It was the *ahu*, the sacred taboo prayer, during which the slightest noise—a dog barking, a rooster crowing, a baby crying—meant instant death to the offender. The chanting by the kahuna would continue all night, as the bones were broken, the body dismembered and burnt, and then the bones defleshed. The people would huddle in their hales, frozen with fear, ready to place their hands over the mouths of their children to muffle their cries, if the children should call out in their sleep. All light was extinguished; no fires could light the terror of darkness, except the torches of the heiau.

Now anguish seized her when she remembered the perfect body of her young lover. What was the meaning of this, that last night she had held him warm and close in a

105

love embrace, and he had breathed sweetness into her hair, and whispered love into her ear, and this night he would be carved like a pig and become a bundle of silent bones? Last night he was *iwi koko*, bloody bones, alive; tonight he was *iwi koko 'ole*, bones without blood. How had it happened?

In a moment of sublime self-truth, the queen looked into the mirror of herself, where she had never looked before. She knew it was she herself who had caused the boy's death, for it was she who had enticed him, it was she who had teased him with her eyes and hips, and it was she who had invited him to her body. Because of her jealousy, her insecurity, her selfishness, because of her intoxication, and most of all because of her indifference to his fate, he had died an untimely and ignominious death.

Only last night she had felt young and innocent again; tonight she knew she was forever old. On the altar where the boy lay, her blamelessness was sacrificed forever.

She looked up; one luminous star in all the dark sky was shining directly over the heiau, the outline of which was silhouetted now by flaming torches. The light of the solitary star was so bright that the breeze-swaying branches of the palm trees that surrounded the heiau could be seen. The vision was so beautiful and lovely, and the lonely sound of the waves lapping upon the deserted shore so exquisite, that she began to weep quietly. And as have all the people of her race done, since time began, when confronting unbearable sorrow, she began to chant, and the mele came spontaneously from her heart and she rocked back and forth on the sand.

"Hear my gentle tears fall, hear my love, hear my gentle tears fall, like rain," she chanted softly, and the tears did fall from her liquid brown eyes onto the sand as she looked up at the temple.

"Hear my gentle tears fall, hear my love, hear my gentle tears fall, like rain," and the sorrowful sound of her words wafted up into the night, intertwined with the eerie sound of the kahuna's chanting to the gods, and the pahu began to beat again very, very slowly.

Long into the dark night, lost in her grief, she continued to sit and chant, and even when she heard the winds rise and the tide change, she continued to sit and chant and mourn. And the night winds became cool and blew harder, and the breaking waves grew louder and louder and when at last she had no more tears, and her storm of grief had subsided, a fiery hot anger came upon her. She clenched a handful of damp sand in her hand and squeezed hard.

"I will destroy him," she said to herself. "I will turn his own son against him. I will sway the wills of the mightiest warriors against him. The people will obey me, and all shall rebel against him. All that he has won shall be lost. Even the gods shall turn their back on him."

And to him she said, "You will be assassinated in the dark."

And then a hard, cold hatred settled in her *iwi kani*, her strong bones.

She sat without moving, though the chill night air became damp, thinking of the revenge she would visit upon her king. Every detail of his death she plotted, and she gleefully envisioned his ignominious end, to his very bones.

"Your bones shall not be able to hide. Your bones shall be fish hooks," she said to him, and she laughed aloud vindictively. "Eels and sharks shall bite your bones."

With the thought of the king's bones as fishhooks, she saw him in her mind's eye. She saw him as she had seen him the first time, when she was but a child—a huge, giant of a man with a terrible, frowning visage, a heavy brow already furrowed with the weight of his lonely secrets. She pictured him again when, she still a child, they had

107

made love on the marriage mat for the first time, their thighs rejoicing, and she saw herself tracing the deep lineaments of his ponderous face with her fingers as she lay beneath him. She saw again, how, with the touch of her innocent, trusting, playful fingers, his lonely face had softened. Unaccustomed to smiling, he had smiled at her the only way he could, with his bright eyes, and she had smiled brightly back.

"Lokomaika'i" she had whispered softly. "I see that you are filled with kindness."

And his eyes had watered with love, so that she encircled her arms about him like a lei.

That was the moment in which they had truly become man and wife.

She saw him, as he was now, old, his great shoulders beginning to stoop slightly, his proud footstep beginning to shuffle, his hair beginning to turn white. His frowning, creased face wore the look of fierceness and loneliness it had always worn, but when had his eyes become so sad and lusterless? Why had she not noticed before?

"Yes," she thought sadly. "So it is. Even iwi kani, even the strong bones of a king such as this, grow old and feeble."

At the thought of her king's bones grown old and feeble, at the thought of his decline, the sorrow of their great love welled up in her and she thought, "Oh, to think soon you will be gone. Oh, to think of being apart from you! Oh, my beloved. *Hoa pakau noho'i i I ke aloha.* Companion upon whom my love rests."

The pahu stopped beating; the eerie chant of the kahuna ceased, and in their stead, she heard the thundering sound of the crashing waves of the sea pounding the shore. She looked up and saw blood red streaks of the first light of dawn directly over the heiau. It was a new day.

The priest came from out of the heiau, carrying the king's standard of feathers, and he lifted it to the sky as he

108

loudly called out, so that the people crouching in their hales could hear, "*Noa noa*, the taboo is lifted."

For a few moments more, all was still quiet, then, very slowly, a drift of voices could be heard in all directions, as the people began to emerge from their hales. Children's laughter sounded as they ran from their mother's arms; the sound of discontented babies wailing for their morning food could also be heard. Dogs began to bark, roosters began to crow. It was a new day; life began to flow again, as it always did, because the gods were satisfied.

Wakea had eaten.

A great wave crashed on the shore behind her, and someone happily shouted, "*Nalu kua loloa*!" "Long wave!"

She stood and stretched. Her bones were stiff with sitting all night in the cold air. Turning toward the sea, she saw that indeed the waves were long, perfect waves.

"Nalu kua loloa," she shouted happily, and she ran across the beach, dove into a crashing wave, and swam as fast as a dolphin toward the cresting sea.

*

And it was as she had thought—soon enough, in a very short time, her beloved king died. *I ka make 'ana o kana kane, ua ho'olaua'e a'ela 'oia ike aloha*—at the death of her husband, she cherished the loving memory.

"Oh," she cried, inconsolably, "if only once again I could warm his bones."

And very soon thereafter, a little ship sailed in carrying foreign men and women skilled in a strangely magical art of alphabets and symbols, and the quick-witted queen was the first in the land to learn to read and write.

And upon her inner thigh, which had once encircled her king like a lei, she had written forever, with a needle

109

made from the beak of a bird, and black ink from the ashes of kukui nut and charred fish bones, the word, "*Auhea*," "Where has he gone?"

****

BONES OF LOVE

Puanani, "Beautiful Flower," was not old, but she had been ill for many days, and now it was certain that she lay dying. She was the wife of the fisherman and farmer Lihau, whose name betokened both the cool gentle rain that was lucky for those who wore their malo in the sea, the fishermen, and the fresh, dew-laden breeze that moistened the earth. Now Lihau, his two sons and daughter and the seven grandchildren sat around the mat, grieving, for Puanani had been a good mother and grandmother, but most of all she had been a good wife, and Lihau loved her dearly. He was a quiet man, and did not express his feelings openly, but now he was anguished; he did not know how he could live without her, his beautiful flower.

For many days, as she had grown weaker and weaker, he would not believe that she could die, that she could leave him. Indeed, were they not both in the prime of their lives? Were they not to live to see many more flowers blossom from their union—grandchildren and great-grandchildren and great-great grandchildren? It was unthinkable that she should die. He had sent for the *kahuna lapa'au*, the healer. He had made every offering to the family gods, the 'aumakua, for the recovery of his cherished wife. He had chanted the *pule he'e*, the prayer to *he'e*, the octopus, as it lay on the ocean floor being tempted by the cowry hook, and when it was caught, the he'e was offered to the deity, but still his wife had declined, and at last the kahuna lapa'au said it was her time.

Puanani opened her eyes and looked directly at her husband, and, with supreme effort, she lifted her arms up, as if to embrace him. When he realized what she was trying to do, he forgot his shyness and leaned forward with his arms open also, but, alas, it was too late; she fell back on the mat, and she was gone. He was cheated of a last embrace. The grandchildren screamed, the daughter and daughters-in-law began to wail, and the sons quietly began to weep, but Lihau sat like a stone, with his hand over his wife's hand, which would soon grow cold.

The *kaumaha*, the grief of the family, was great. The sons chanted the ritual prayers all day long, offering bananas, coconuts, and *awa* to honor the lizard god Kaio'e, while the women continued to wail and chant through the hours, and still Lihau sat near his wife, unmoving and stricken. The little children were frightened and their mothers tried to explain to them that grandmother was going to become an 'aumakua, a family god. They came and sat quietly beside Lihau, starring at grandmother; grandmother lay silent and motionless until the youngest child leaned over her to get a closer look— the eyes of the corpse suddenly flew open and the children shrieked in terror and fled.

The illogical thought quickly came into Lihau's mind that his wife was, after all, not dead, and he leaned forward and whispered, "Puanani?"

But Puanani only stared back him with expressionless, glassy eyes, until someone, Lihau did not notice who, came and gently closed the eyes and put small, flat, grey stones on the eyelids, so that the face of the corpse resembled somewhat a big-eyed mo'o, a lizard, which was, after all, the family 'aumakua. After one look, the children refused to go near again. Lihau continued to sit by his wife's side, as though he too were dead, while one by one the family members came forward and spoke their feelings to Puanani, telling of their love, and of her kindness.

When the lamentations had ended, Lihau at last roused himself to perform his religious duties, because he was *makua kane*, father of the household. He moved about as in a dream, looking at no one. When all the death rituals had been completed perfectly and it was time for the *puholoholo*, the steaming of the corpse, he lifted his wife, now wrapped in ti and banana leaves, and carried her cold body tenderly to the pit. After the *holehole iwi*, the stripping of the bones of flesh, it was he who so tenderly laid the bones upon the kapa cloth, the finest they had, wrapped them into a neat bundle and placed them at the *kua'aha*, the family altar. When that was done, it was he alone who carried her flesh and organs in a calabash and rowed his canoe far out to sea, where he sank them into the deep waters, to be devoured by the creatures of the inky depths.

The *'aha'aina make*, the feast of death, was held, the gods were fed, and all the family and friends took part, but Lihau sat without eating. Lihau's children were concerned for him, because he shed no tears, and he did not eat. His daughter tried to coax him with his favorite foods, but he only said that he had no hunger, and got up and left his friends and family. No one knew where he had gone, until one of the little children said that grandfather was sitting beside the iwi, the bones.

After that, one early morning when the river was low, and the coming night would be a night of full moon, Lihau, carefully carrying the bundle of bones, with all his children and their children following him, except the smallest children, trudged across the valley. Cautiously they waded the river, and slowly and laboriously climbed the *pali*, the steep almost inaccessible cliff over the sea, to the hidden cave of the ancestors, the *lua pao*. Hand-over-

113

hand they climbed, high above the dizzying sea below. Before the mouth of the cave was a large overhanging shelf of rock; upon it was carved a huge centipede-type creature, a *kanapi*. Here, the family paused and rested while the two sons made a fire with wood one had carried on his back. When the fire was strong, they lit torches of kukui-nut oil and handed one to Lihau, who, holding the torch with one hand, and the bundle of bones with the other, led the way into the dark opening of the cave.

They were greeted by a cold draught of air that carried a strong, musty odor of decay, as if it came from the very bowels of the earth. From the innermost recesses of the darkness, a faint high-pitched whistling sound seemed to be warning against trespassing against the dead. The children, too afraid to cry, or even speak, pressed up closely against their mothers, and the women pressed up closely against their men. Lihau walked very, very slowly forward, holding the torch high, while making a slow, sweeping motion with the fire. He could be heard murmuring, as if he were counting his paces, which he was. After a certain number of steps, he paused and slowly lifted the torch to his right and left.

"It is I, Lihau, come with my wife, my children, and my children's children," announced Lihau, in a strong voice, and his words resounded as a cavernous echo, "It is I, Lihau. It is I, Lihau. It is I, Lihau," before slowly dying away in the dark depths of the cave.

In the eerie circle of light illumined by the torch, on a kind of ledge built of stones along each of the cave walls, stood rows of moldy, decomposing and putrid kapa bundles, similar to the bundle he carried now. Lihau began to step slowly forward again, counting his paces, with all the family following in single file, one son carrying the torch behind.

When Lihau stopped again, and held his torch high in front of him, a stone idol of indefinite shape except for two

114

indented cavities that were unmistakably eyes, stared back. Lihau motioned for the family to come closer, and as he slowly illuminated the ancient family altar, wooden gods on sticks and strange-shaped beings of stone, some with tails, seemed to come alive in the shadows of the flickering flames. Lihau motioned for the son who was carrying the offerings, wrapped in ti leaves, to come forward, and these were placed on the altar, as Lihau chanted the *pule kahea*, the prayer calling the family gods, the ʻaumakua. From some distant place in the far darkness, an echo, or an ancestor, chanted back. Lihau finished chanting, and the peculiar high-pitched whistling stopped abruptly. That was good—the offering had been accepted. All was absolutely silent now, for the gods were eating.

Lihau silently motioned for the family to follow him. As he walked slowly back toward the entrance of the cave, from which a faint strange green light streamed, giving the effect that they were all underwater, he stopped before each kapa bundle, calling the name of each ancestor, and telling, for the sake of his children and his children's children, stories of their lives. Near his own father and mother, he tenderly placed the bones of his wife.

"My bones will rest here," he said to his sons and daughter, and he lovingly patted with his palm the place next to the bones of his wife. "And your bones," he said to the wide-eyed grandchildren, pointing to a place on the shelf, "will rest here." And then he motioned for the family to follow him outside.

When they had emerged again into the crystal blue daylight, they sat together on the ledge eating their food, taking pleasure in the sun, and in the fragrance of life, the smell of the salt sea that wafted up from below. Lihau took this time to warn the grandchildren never to speak of the ancestral cave to outsiders, and especially, never, never to speak of the ʻaumakua, the family gods.

"This," said Lihau, and he traced with his finger the lines of the kanapi which was carved on the rock shelf, "is our family. These legs, these segments, are our family. This body is the backbone of our family; all our ancestors are here."

Lihau related how, twenty years ago, the King had ordered the destruction of all the temples of the akua, the ancient gods, and forbidden the worship of the 'aumakua. Lihau, who was submissive to the King, but who honored and feared the gods, had been confounded, until one night, he had an *ho'ike a ka po*, a revelation from the gods, which told him to hide the 'aumakua. Lihau, without hesitation, had secretly carried the 'aumakua, the stone image with the vacant eyes, and the gods on sticks, to the cave of the ancestors.

Now Lihau, who was a man of few words, gazed out over the sea, and spoke solemnly, for his children and grandchildren and their children must never forget. He spoke of the *leina-a-ka-'uhane*, the leap of the soul, the place where the spirits of men and women, at the time of death, leaped into the sea of all space and time, into eternity and infinity, which is called the sea of Po. In Po, Lihau explained, dwell all the ancestors since time began, the ancestors who have been transfigured by spirit magic into "aumakua, the family gods who looked after and protected their descendants with loving care. But, warned Lihau, sternly, the 'aumakua must be revered; they must be loved and fed. And their bones must be cared for.

"Do you understand?" asked Lihau. And all the family nodded solemnly.

"Do you understand?" asked Lihau, of his smallest grandson.

"Yes," said the boy, "we take care of the gods, and the gods take care of us."

Lihau smiled, for the boy had understood.

116

The family began to ready themselves for the return home. Lihau's children were surprised and concerned when Lihau told them that he planned to stay at the cave for three days.

"Do not be concerned for me," he said, and because he was makua kane, and because they always obeyed, and because they understood that he was grieving, they left him some dried fish, and went on without him. He watched as they very carefully descended the pali, clutching the cliff as they felt with their feet for the next foothold, and he watched from his high place on the ledge over the sea as they wended their way toward home again. Then he relit his torch and went back into the cave, to the bones of his wife, his beautiful flower.

He sat on the cold floor of the cave and was for a while lost in thought, for, after all, he was a man who spoke little. At last he said softly, "Puanani, I, your husband Lihau, am here."

Lihau paused, and then he began again. "Do you remember, Puanani, how we used to play together when we were only so tall?" he asked her, and he began to recount their early days together, for they were cousins, and from before they could remember, they had always been together.

"Do you remember the time…," he would begin, and then he would remind her of some amusing incident they had experienced together. He would chuckle aloud, then he would remember another humorous incident of their young lives together, and relate it, and in this way, some hours passed.

The torch went out, and the only illumination was the faint green light from the opening of the cave, which was now the light of the moon, but Lihau continued to sit before his wife's bones. He talked to her of when they had grown older, and had become sweethearts, and of how

117

they had shyly begun to plan their lives together, for they had always known they would always be together.

"Do you remember," he asked, "the first day you came to live with me? Do you remember how the kalo sparkled in the field in the summer sun as we walked the path to my house? Do you remember the white shimmering light of the morning? That day everything sparkled."

Then he became quiet, and waited for her to speak, for there were some things, he, being a reticent man, he could not say.

"'U, yes," the bones of his wife spoke softly. "I am listening. I remember all these things. I too remember that early morning I came to live with you, that everything sparkled. I too remember how the path to your house glittered, for we walked upon dewdrops, hand in hand.

There was a long silence, as they both recalled the cherished memory.

The bones of his wife spoke again. "Do you remember our marriage night, the first time we lay on the marriage mat together?"

"'U, yes," said Lihau. "'*Elua kaua i ke kapa ho'okahi*. Two of us in a single kapa."

"'U, yes," the bones of his wife spoke in a whisper. "Do you remember how the rain fell in fine mist all the night long? Do you remember what you called me?"

There was another long silence, for Lihau well remembered, but he could not say the words, for he was too shy to speak his innermost feelings.

"You called me *ku'u aloha*. Beloved," said the bones.

Lihau could not speak for a long time. At last, he said, "After that, after that night, you became very shy."

"So did you," said the bones of his wife. Then the bones said, coquettishly, "Why did you choose me?"

"Because," said Lihau, "when we were small, you and I would always laugh together. To laugh is good. As a woman, you were shy and kind. Also, you don't talk too much," he added, teasingly. "And why did you choose me?"

"Same here," answered the bones, also teasingly.

Both Lihau and the bones of his wife chuckled.

In this way, Lihau and the bones of his wife talked throughout the night. When daylight came, Lihau followed the green light to the opening of the cave, sat in the sunshine, and ate some dried fish, while he gazed out over the deep blue sea. Then he lay down on the sun-warmed shelf, on the kanapi drawn on the rock, and slept.

When Lihau had refreshed himself, he again made a fire, lit the torch, and entered the cave, where he sat on the ground and talked to the bones of his wife. In this way, three days and nights passed.

"Goodbye, Puanani," said Lihau, on the last morning. "I will return soon."

But the bones of his wife said nothing, and with a last gentle pat on the bundle, Lihau departed reluctantly, for he was grieved to leave his wife.

When Lihau returned home, he spoke to no one but went straight to work in the kalo field. Lihau's children knew that this was his way, and left him alone, for they understood he was suffering. It was in the evening, in the dark as they all sat by the fire, that they heard it, a strange wailing sound coming from the sea cliffs and carried over the valley.

"Do you hear that wind?" asked Lihau's daughter, and they all listened.

"I have never heard a wind like that before," said one of the sons.

"There is no wind," said the other son. "Look for yourself. The tree branches do not move."

"That is no wind," said Lihau, without looking up, "that is the crying of your mother."

119

The others could say nothing, for it was a fact; there was no wind.

For three nights, as soon as dark descended, the strange crying could be heard until daybreak; each night, the plaintive cry sounded more and more anguished, so that those who heard it could scarcely bear to listen. They discussed it, and though they all knew it was not the wind, they called it "the crying on the wind." On the fourth day, Lihau, without saying a word, departed across the valley. His children watched him go.

He crossed the river, collected firewood that he carried on his back, and climbed the cliff to the cave, where he made a fire and lit a torch. As before, he entered the cave and heard the faint high-pitched whistling, and he counted his paces to the altar of his gods.

"It is I, Lihau," he announced in a strong voice. "I have come alone."

Then, as before, he made offerings to the gods, and chanted the prayer. Then, as before, the whistling sound ceased, for the gods were eating. Lihau retraced his steps to the bones of his wife.

"It is I, Lihau, your husband," he said. "I have heard you crying, Puanani. You must not cry."

In this way, Lihau spoke to the bones of his wife, to comfort her. For some hours, he sat on the floor of the cave and talked to her. At last, he reassured her that he would return often.

"Goodbye, Puanani," said Lihau, but the bones of his wife were silent.

Lihau departed, as before, retracing his steps to the mouth of the cave, from which green light poured, and again, it seemed as if somehow, all of this, the ancestral cave with the bones of the 'aumakua, was underwater.

That evening, as before, when darkness descended, the sorrowful cry on the wind, though there was no wind, could be heard, and before morning, it had become so

120

anguished, that the family began to speak of seeking the help of a kahuna, a priest who understood these things.

"We must be able to sleep at night," protested one son, "or we cannot work during the day."

"No, no," said Lihau, and again he crossed the valley, climbed to the cave, and as before, spoke to the bones of his wife, to comfort her. As before, when he said goodbye, the bones of his wife were silent.

That evening, at home again, when darkness descended, the inconsolable wailing on the wind, though there was no wind, was heard. No one could sleep for the sadness of it, and the children cried in fear.

In the morning, Lihau gathered a calabash, crossed the river and the valley, and climbed to the cliff. As before, he prayed to his gods, and fed them. Then he stood before the bones of his wife.

"Puanani," he said, "it is I, Lihau, your husband. I have come to take you home."

Lihau carefully opened the bundle of bones and removed one bone, which he lovingly wrapped in ti leaves and placed in the calabash. He tenderly rewrapped the bundle and placed it on the shelf, then retraced his steps to the mouth of the cave, descended the cliff, and headed home.

When Lihau returned home, he said nothing to anyone. Taking the bone from the calabash and wrapping it in kapa, he placed it under his sleeping mat. One of the grandchildren saw him.

"Lihau has something hidden under his mat," he told the others.

"Not your *kuleana*," said the mother, "not your concern," but she looked at her husband.

That evening, when darkness fell, the family waited, expectantly, for the crying on the wind, but the evening was quiet, and the family slept peacefully through the night, the little children entwined in the arms and legs of their mothers and fathers, and the breastbone of Puanani beneath the head of her husband.

*

Three full moons passed, and Lihau gathered a calabash, into which he placed the breastbone of his wife, wrapped in kapa, and announced that he was going to the ancestral cave for a day and a night.

"To clean the bones," he said.

As before, he paid homage to his gods. Then he took the breastbone of his wife from the calabash, unwrapped it from the ti leaves, and placed it with the other bones of Puanani. As before, he sat on the floor and spoke to the bones of his wife. He said nothing to her of her death, however, but he talked of life, and the many things they had shared, for they had shared almost everything.

"Do you remember when our first son was born?" asked Lihau. "That was a happy day."

"'U, yes, I remember," spoke the bones of his wife. "That was a happy day."

"I remember how difficult it was for you," said Lihau, hesitantly, for he was not given to express his innermost feelings readily, and he had had great fear for her. "You almost died."

"'Yes," said the bones of his wife, "I remember how you tenderly looked at me before you even looked at the child. You said, 'Ku'u aloha. Beloved.'"

Lihau felt shy and said nothing, but smiled at this memory.

Lihau slept on the floor of the cave, near the bones of his wife, which he had cleaned until they shone, and in the morning, after wrapping her breastbone carefully in the kapa again, and placing it in his calabash, he departed for home.

Another three full moons passed and again Lihau announced that he was going to the ancestral cave for a day and a night.

"To clean the bones," he said, and he slung his calabash across his shoulder.

His sons and daughter looked at one another but said nothing, for they knew their father was grieving hard.

Again three full moons passed and again Lihau announced that he was going to the ancestral cave to clean the bones.

His daughter ventured to say, "But you just cleaned the bones. It cannot be that they need cleaning so soon."

Lihau looked at her wrathfully and she dared say nothing more. He crossed the river and the valley, carrying the calabash with the breastbone, climbed the pali, and visited the bones of his wife as before, talking with her of the life they had shared together.

Now a full year had passed since the death of Lihau's wife, and it was the time for the *'aha'aina waimaka*, the feast of tears. All the family and friends gathered for food and laughter, for the time of grieving had ended. For them, but not for Lihau. He gathered his calabash and headed for the cave of the ancestors, for his grief, and his love for Puanani, his beautiful flower, as long as his bones had blood, would never end.

"I am going to clean the bones," he said, and everyone looked at him in silence.

*

In this way, every few full moons, Lihau crossed the river and the valley and climbed to the cave of the ancestors to "clean the bones." Time passed, and Lihau only became more silent and withdrawn. Once, and one time only, when one of his sons jokingly mentioned that his father, still being handsome and strong, could get a new young wife, Lihau gave such a withering, scowling look that no one ever dared again to hint or jest that he might remarry.

"Lihau is content to sleep with his bone," they said behind his back, and laughed.

A first great-grandchild was born, and then another, and another, and as in the old days, all the family, the *ohana nui*, lived together, working the land, fishing, paying tribute to the king.

But an event happened that would change the ancient way of life, indeed, the life of the entire race of ancient people, forever. The family did not understand right away; years would pass before they knew. It happened the same year that the first great-grandchild of Lihau and Puanani was born.

It was the Great Mahele. The land upon which the family had lived and worked was sold from beneath them. But they did not know or understand, and for some years, they continued to live as before, unaffected by the doings of strangers and a king who lived on distant shores.

*

Years passed and with them, changes occurred. The great-grandchildren walked to the village to a school, where they were told to speak in the language of the haoles, the white men, and taught to address their grandparents and great-grandparents fondly as "Kuku." Lihau, now an old man, did not approve of this, and insisted on being called by the name his parents had given him, as in the old times. When the children called him Kuku, he refused to answer.

"My name is Lihau," he would say, indignantly, and he would draw up his thinning shoulders and his beginning-to-stoop back, proudly.

Though he now walked with a limp, and his stride was slow, every few moons Lihau, with his wife's breastbone in the calabash, would cross the river and the valley, and very slowly climb the pali to the ancestral cave, to feed the gods, clean the bones, and talk with his wife.

One day some haoles, white men, came and told them to leave their land. Lihau and his family protested, but it was no use; their hales, their houses made of pili grass, were torn down, their kalo fields were torn up, and they were made to go. They walked to a not-so-distant village, carrying their possessions.

Lihau's anger was huge, but his sorrow was even greater, for what of the ancestral cave? What of the 'aumakua? What of the bones of his wife?

"No one is ever to speak of the cave of the ancestors to others," said Lihau, fiercely, to his ohana.

He had one consolation—the cave was so inaccessible; it would never be discovered by the strangers. He himself could continue to walk—however slowly, for he was an old man now—the few miles from the village, and on a full moon night, when no one was watching, he could climb the pali to the cave of the ancestors.

In the village, Lihau's grandsons worked for strangers and the family lived in a house made of wood. Lihau's hair grew white, his teeth began to fall out, and his hearing faded. The first great family difficulty occurred when Lihau's daughter died. Her children, Lihau's grandchildren, arranged, without consulting him, for her to be buried in the new way, in the ground. Lihau was horrified, but in the end, powerless, and the grandchildren had their way.

"In the ground. Like pigs," said Lihau, and he shook his head at the sadness of it.

On the full moon following this, Lihau surreptitiously climbed the pali with his offerings and his calabash. He dared not speak to the gods of his daughter's bones, that they lay in the earth, for shame, and he could not speak of them to the bones of his wife, for kindness of her feelings.

When descending the pali, he slipped and hurt his leg badly, so that he had great difficulty crossing the river. Not only that, but a stranger, on his own land, a *luna*, the haole overseer, saw him, accosted him, and said "*'Ae'a haukea'e*, vagrant, trespasser! If you come here again, we will put the dogs on you!"

When he finally returned to his family in the village, clutching his calabash that carried the breastbone of his wife, he was shaking with cold. He was put to bed by one of his grandchildren, and no one thought he would live the night.

"I have something to say, for I am uneasy," whispered Lihau, to the granddaughter, and she had the family gather around—Lihau and Puanani's children, and grandchildren, and great-grand-children, because they believed he was dying.

"*'Ma'ane 'iau me 'oe a waiho na iwi*," whispered Lihau, "here I am with you until leaving the bones. I thank you for caring for me, an old man now. I am uneasy, and will be uneasy for all time, until you promise that my iwi, my bones, shall be returned to the cave of our ancestors."

The family soothed the old man with promises that it would be as he desired and directed, and he went to sleep peacefully with the breastbone of his wife beneath the pillow.

But Lihau did not die that night, or the next. Though very ill, he slowly recuperated, but the wound on his leg did not completely heal and he could only walk with a cane, and his former strength did not return. Nevertheless, when a few months had passed, he gathered his calabash for his visit to the cave of the ancestors. When the family saw what he was doing, they looked at one another.

126

"You cannot go again, you are too old," they told him gently, but he angrily brushed away the loving hands they placed on his shoulders, and hobbled down the village street. He did not go far however, before he fell, and his calabash rolled down the street. He and his calabash had to be carried back by his great-grandsons. After that, he could never walk again, for he had broken his hip.

Lihau lay in his bed, year after year. His two sons died, and great-great-grandchildren were born. It was a granddaughter and a great-granddaughter who cared for his needs, fed him and bathed him, but mostly he lay as in a deep dream with closed eyes, while the world went on without him. The great-granddaughter, who had been taught in the new ways, did not like the idea of the bone in the bed. This created a family disturbance, and at last a compromise was reached—the bone was placed in the calabash and set on a pretty chest before the bed, so that "Kuku," as she insisted on calling Lihau, in the new way, since he couldn't hear her anyway, could see it. The bone was a great comfort to Lihau.

One day, Lihau became aware that two boys were in the room where he lay. One was his great-great-grandson; the other, a *kolohe*, a mischief-maker, with eyes like a rat.

"Who is this old *pu'u welu*, this old heap of rags?" asked the kolohe, and he walked over and looked down at the old man, who was unable to move or speak, but who looked up at the kolohe with dim eyes.

"I'm not sure," said the great-great-grandson. "He's just always been here."

The kolohe bent down in the old man's face and stuck out his tongue. "Hey! Old molar tooth yellow with age!" he shouted into the old man's ear.

The great-great-grandson laughed. Then the kolohe went to the foot of the bed and uncovered Lihau's feet.

"How do you like this, old bag of bones?" said the kolohe, and he began tickling one of the old man's feet.

As Lihau could do nothing, since he could move nothing but his eyes, he tried to glare at the boy.

"I think he likes it, don't you?" said the kolohe to the great-great-grandson, "See how he is looking at us." And he began to tickle both feet, and the two boys laughed.

The mean boy soon, however, lost interest in the old man's feet, and began to look around the room for some other way to misbehave. He spotted the calabash on the pretty chest. The old man followed him with his eyes.

"Say, what's this?" the kolohe said, and he reached into the calabash and pulled out something wrapped in old kapa cloth.

"That's his," said the great-great-grandchild, pointing to the old man, who watched from his bed, with imploring eyes. "I'm not supposed to touch it."

"Is that right?" said the kolohe, with an evil smile on his face. "Well, let's see what it is."

The old man, lying in his bed, tried to scream out; with supreme effort, his toothless mouth moved up and down and sideways, but no words would come.

The kolohe roughly shook the kapa cloth, and the breastbone of Lihau's wife rolled out and onto the floor.

"Hey look, it's a bone!" said the kolohe, and the two boys walked over and squatted near the bone.

"Sure is shiny," said the great-great-grandson.

"It's old, too," said the kolohe.

"How do you know?" asked the great-great-grandson.

"Look!" said the kolohe. He stood up and with one foot stomped on the breastbone of Lihau's wife. It shattered into pieces.

"It's old all right," said the great-great-grandson. "But now what? When my father finds out…"

"*'A'ole pilikia, no problem*," said the kolohe, and he picked up the pieces of bones and stashed them in his pocket. "I'll throw these to the dogs."

"I don't think dogs will eat old bones like that," said the great-great-grandson, doubtfully.

"Well, at least they will chew them up real good," said the kolohe.

The kolohe then squeezed the kapa cloth into a bundle and stuffed it into the calabash. As they left the room, they turned to close the door. The kolohe took a last indifferent look at the old man who lay on the bed, his eyes streaming with tears.

*

When Lihau's great-granddaughter came in to check on him, she mistook the distraught and grieved face of the old man for physical pain.

"What is it, Kuku? she asked, as if she were talking to a little child, or one who was not of right mind. Of course, being unable to speak, Lihau could not answer. She sat beside him on the bed and asked him other questions, which of course he could not answer, and finally, after tucking covers high up around his neck, though it was not cold, she told him good night, and that she knew he would feel better in the morning. To the family, however, she said that Kuku did not look well, and she didn't know how he could make it to the morning.

*

When she had gone, Lihau shut his eyes and looked within. With anguish, he realized more than ever before that the only thing he wanted and had wanted was to be in the cave of the ancestors with the bones of his wife. It was what he had been waiting for so many years of his life. It was all that mattered and it was what he had expected. He had prayed and made offering to the gods; he had fed

129

them, and he had polished the bones of his ancestors with trust and love.

He now saw for the first time that perhaps, after all, these people would not return his bones to the ancestral home. Now he saw that perhaps his wishes meant nothing to these people—his grandchildren, and great-grandchildren, and great-great-grandchildren. They would, perhaps, bury him too in the earth, like pig bones. For them, the 'aumakua were not real.

Now Lihau realized that only the gods could give him this thing he wanted. In the agony of his pain, but in his trust, he called on his gods.

"It is I, Lihau," he called inwardly. "I have come alone," and immediately, there was a feeling as if he were falling, as if he were rushing headfirst into darkness, and away he plunged into a black abyss.

When Lihau opened his eyes, he stood again at the ancient altar in the cave of the ancestors. The stone god stared back at him with vacant eyes, and the gods on sticks seemed to dance in the flickering light of the torch he held in one hand. A high-pitched whistling warned against trespassing and Lihau examined himself, and found himself honest, and his life true, and his trust real. He looked without fear straight at the gods, and he made his offerings and he chanted the *pule kahea*, the prayer to the gods. When the chant ended, the whistling died away; all was silent, and that was good; the gods were eating.

Lihau turned from the altar, and on the faint green light, which streamed from the opening of the cave, he floated away, into Po, the infinite and eternal sea of time.

In the valley that had once been the land of Lihau and his ancestors, the haole luna and his wife were just sitting down to dinner.

"What a wind!" his wife exclaimed. "I have never heard a wind like that before. It sounds like a woman crying."

"There is no wind. Just look, not a tree leaf is moving," said the luna, and he looked out across the valley, toward the pali from where the wailing sound came.

"Whatever is it, then?" asked his wife, but the luna could not answer.

*

Lihau's great-granddaughter was right—Lihau did not live until morning. Now the family had a problem. The great-grandchildren and their husbands and wives, and two of the grandchildren wished to have Kuku buried in the ground, in the new way, with a stone marker. But the oldest grandson, now almost an old man himself, had a worry in his mind. He remembered as a child going to the cave of the ancestors, and he clearly remembered how Lihau had patted the stone shelf next to his wife's bones, and said, "My bones will go here." He also remembered clearly how the family had promised the old man that his bones would be returned to the cave. He also remembered a certain question a little boy had once been asked, sitting high up on a ledge over the sea, tracing with his finger the lines of a kanapi. He alone insisted that the old man's wishes must be respected.

"But Father," said the great-granddaughter, "who will prepare his bones? These things are just not done anymore. Besides, it is not convenient. And would the luna of the old land give consent?"

131

But the grandson insisted. "It is *ho'okupono*; it is to behave uprightly," he said. "I will make the arrangements."

And he did. He knew of one who would prepare the bones of the old man, old style, and he had the body conveyed in a wagon by a horse to the steam pit. He also obtained permission from the luna, on condition that the luna could accompany the family, to return the bones to the cave.

When the luna told his wife, she said, "I don't know. There are strange stories about those burial caves. I don't think you should go."

The luna chuckled and said, "Those stories are hogwash. There are probably valuable artifacts in that cave. Who knows how much they are worth?"

When the bones of the old man, steamed and cleaned, were returned to the family, wrapped in a kapa bundle, old style, the family discussed how the bones would be returned to the cave of the ancestors.

"Let's all go, we can have a pikiniki," suggested the great-granddaughter.

A day was chosen for the return of the bones, and the great-granddaughter invited friends of the family for the fun. The great-great-grandchild, hearing this, asked if he could invite his friend, and so in this way, the kolohe, the mischief-maker with the eyes of a rat, once again was involved with Lihau.

*

On the day of the picnic, the family gathered with great baskets of food, and there was much merriment and anticipation of spending the day doing something unusual. The grandson gathered the bones of his grandfather, wrapped in the kapa cloth, and put them in one of the picnic baskets with the food, and the family was ready to

132

leave when the great-granddaughter remembered Kuku's bone. She went to the calabash and pulled out the kapa cloth, but of course, there was no bone.

"The old fool has lost his bone," announced the great-granddaughter to the gathered family and friends.

"Hush. Do not talk about Kuku that way," said her father, but, just the same, everyone laughed. The great-great-grandson, and the kolohe, who were listening, said nothing, but grinned broadly at one another.

The family and friends rode in wagons to the land that had once belonged to Lihau and his ancestors. The luna, with a friend of his own, was waiting for them. Carrying the baskets of food and the bones of Lihau, with much gaiety and laughter, the group crossed the river and valley, and came to the bottom of the pali.

"I don't see any cave," said the luna.

Nor could anyone else see a cave.

"It's there, where you see the overhanging ledge, above the sea," said the grandfather. "It's hidden."

The women looked with anxiety at the steep pali and declined to climb it, or let the children go. At this, the great-great-grandson and the kolohe began to yowl, until finally the women agreed the boys could go but not the girls. The luna and his friend, who also were nervous, but didn't wish to be grouped with the women, and who also had the great desire to see what valuables might be in the cave, voiced a false enthusiasm. Grandfather really didn't wish to climb, but being the only one who had been there before, and who knew where the bones were to be placed, he reluctantly made ready. The women began to spread a lunch at the base of the pali, and the men and boys began the climb, carrying lanterns slung on their backs.

The group of men climbed slowly, with Grandfather in the lead, and the two boys in the middle. They climbed carefully—all, of course, except the kolohe, who was reckless—but just the same, loose rocks and bits of dirt fell to the sea below as they grabbed for handholds and footholds, for no one had climbed the pali for many years. When they were all safely on the ledge, they expressed sighs of relief, except the kolohe, who stood at the very edge of the cliff, so that bits of it crumbled to the sea below, and shouted to his mother, pointing to himself and laughing. Then he bent and picked up a stone, yelped, and threw it at her. From far below, she could be seen pointing at him and shouting something back, but what she shouted could not be heard.

"What's this?" asked the friend of the luna, as he stared at the ancient kanapi drawn on the ledge.

"Looks like a primitive drawing, maybe a stick-figure centipede?" offered the luna.

The kolohe came to see what they were looking at; he stared for a moment, then with great gusto dug his heel into the head of the kanape, so that a piece of it cracked off.

"Watch this!" he bellowed, and he picked up the shard and threw it far out into the sea.

The kolohe took out some crack seed he had in his pocket, and while the men were lighting the lanterns, he ran wildly into the entrance of the cave, but he stopped immediately and shouted, "It's dark in there!" He spat the uneaten pit of the crack seed into the darkness and took out another.

Now the men, carrying the lanterns, entered the cave. A cold draught of musty air that seemed to come from the very bowels of the earth hit them in the face. From the innermost recesses of darkness came a faint high-pitched whistling sound, which caused even the kolohe to stop in his tracks for a moment.

"What's that sound?" he whispered.

"Just the wind," answered the luna.

"I never heard a wind like that before," said the friend of the luna.

The group of men and boys stepped slowly forward, the men warily shining their lanterns to the right and then the left.

"Look!" shouted the kolohe, when they had advanced some paces into the cave,

Against the walls of the cave, on shelves made of stacked stones, were small, mossy kapa bundles. A large spider ducked behind one when one of the men shone a lantern on it.

"Did you see that?" yelled the kolohe, "let me have a lantern!" and he rudely snatched one from the hands of the man who held it, and began boisterously searching for the spider.

The luna let out a long whistle, and exclaimed loudly, "These are old!"

"Invaluable!" exclaimed his friend.

Grandfather led the way slowly, searching right and left, and finally he said, "I think this it. This is where Kuku said to leave his bones."

He shined the lantern on a mildewy bundle of kapa, the bones of Lihau's wife.

"Here you go, Kuku," he said, and he placed the bundle of bones, all that was left of Lihau, wrapped in kapa and ti leaves, on the shelf next to the bundle of bones of Lihau's wife.

Suddenly, from the further reach of the cave, came a wild whoop.

"Look at this! Look at this!" excitedly shouted the kolohe.

The others began to advance quickly toward the light in the distant end of the cave, swinging their lanterns left and right, illuminating decaying bundles, some larger, some smaller, on both sides of the cave. When they reached the kolohe, who stood before the ancient altar, wide-eyed with excitement, they stopped dead in their tracks.

135

A stone idol of peculiar shape, unidentifiable as human or non-human, as male or female, except that it had two indented cavities which seemed to be eyes, stared malevolently back at them. Surrounding the idol, on a bed of something deep green and moldy, strangely carved wooden figures on sticks and smaller stone figures with beady eyes and long tails stood as if sentinels. The eerie whistling sound, which they had heard since they had entered the cave, grew louder, shriller.

"Good God!" exclaimed the luna, and an echo reverberated back to them, from behind the darkness of the altar, from the more inner recesses of the cave, "Good God! Good God! Good God!"

The kolohe danced excitedly from one foot to the other.

"I found it! I found it! It's mine! he yelled wildly, and he reached out his hands to snatch the idol with the malevolent eyes.

At that very moment, there was a tremor and a rumbling, the stone idol shuddered, the cave tilted, and something black and screeching flew from the darkness beyond straight at the face of the kolohe, who screamed in terror and dropped his lantern, which shattered noisily into pieces on the stone floor. The cave shook and shuddered and for a moment, the men and boys were transfixed.

"'Ola'i!" shouted the grandfather. "Earthquake! Run!"

As fast as they could go, the men and boys, with the luna far in front, dashed toward the eerie green light that streamed in from the opening to the cave. The kolohe in his terror stumbled and fell; Grandfather grabbed him by one arm and drug him across the damp floor of the cave. Stones and dirt rained from above, and below, the floor of the cave undulated in waves.

When Grandfather reached the opening to the cave, hauling the screaming kolohe behind him, he stepped out onto the stone ledge, which, to his amazement, seemed to be swaying back and forth, high above the sea. He saw the women far below, looking up with terror on their faces. The others had already started the descent down, climbing feet first and backward as fast they could go, while rocks and debris fell beside them.

"I will go first, and you come behind," yelled grandfather to the kolohe, who stood petrified with fright. As they descended, Grandfather, holding fast with one hand to the pali, had to place each foot of the terrified kolohe into the next step, and inch his way downward and backward, while the pali shook and quavered.

When they neared the bottom, the kolohe let go, falling upon Grandfather, and the two tumbled down the last few feet of the pali. The others ran to help.

Grandfather struggled to his feet, the kolohe lay on the ground trembling and whimpering, and the whole earth shuddered again. There was a great grating noise, and then a cracking sound. Grandfather pointed to the pali, and the terrified onlookers watched as a thundering avalanche of huge stones and dirt rolled from the top of the pali, striking the rock shelf upon which they had stood such a short time before. With a great splitting sound, the entire shelf splintered and broke from the pali and, falling down, down, crashed into the sea. When dirt and dust had settled, and the earth had calmed herself, the pali had become a sheer, barren wall of rock.

*

Inside the cave of the ancestors, all was now still. The stone idol with the indented eyes, the wooden gods on sticks, the lizard-like stone figures with beady eyes and long tails, stared into absolute blackness, for the green light, that had only moments before streamed from the land of the living and had made the cave of the ancestors

137

seem to be at the bottom of the sea, was extinguished forever. The eerie whistling sound grew fainter and fainter and at last died away, for the *'ape 'ape*, the tiny black bats who had so faithfully guarded the 'aumakua against trespassers, flew blind and screaming, into the furthermost reaches of the maze of lava tubes, to find new resting places on the other side of the pali. They would be only the creatures of flesh and blood who would ever again visit the 'aumakua.

The stone ledge upon which the bones of Lihau and the bones of Puanani rested had fallen and shattered. The bundle of bones of Puanani fell to the floor of the cave, and being years old, split, and her bones spilled loose. As fate would have it, or the gods, the kapa bundle of bones that was Lihau fell right on top, so that he covered and protected her, like a mantle. In time, in human time, that is, the dust of the bones of Puanani and Lihau would mingle.

The hush of the dead ruled, until at last, the bones of Lihau spoke softly.

"Puanani?" whispered the bones of Lihau. "It is I, Lihau, your husband."

"'U, yes, I know," whispered the bones of Puanani. "I am listening."

"Puanani," said the bones of Lihau, with great affection, "*Pua mae 'ole*. You are the flower that never fades."

"And you, Lihau," answered the bones of Puanani, with equal fondness, "*Lihau mai nei 'oe*. You are freshly adorned as the cool dew laden plants."

Lihau was silent, for even now, he was shy in expressing his cherished feelings. At last, he spoke again.

"Puanani, do you remember our marriage night, the first time we lay on the marriage mat together?"

"'U, yes," murmured the bones of Puanani. "*'Elua kaua i ke kapa ho'okahi*. Two of us in a single kapa."

"It is now as it was then," whispered the bones of Lihau.

"'U, yes," said the bones of Puanani, "we are two of us in a single kapa."

There was a long, long silence, for both Lihau and Puanani were lost in the beautiful and alluring wonder of it. Then, with ever the tiniest movement, and without the faintest sound, the bones of Lihau shifted ever so slightly, so that he covered the bones of Puanani even more closely, and he whispered, ever so tenderly, for how could he know what other bones might be listening? "Ku'u aloha. My beloved."

****

THIGH BONE

The year was about 1867.

She gazed at the sparkling isle and a delicious shiver of excitement ran up her spine but she didn't know why. Usually she only had that feeling when she thought things she knew she shouldn't be thinking. Thoughts that the good Father would call sin. But now it was not because of what she was thinking but what she was seeing.

The ship had anchored all night offshore, because of the ferocity of the people. She watched as the first light of dawn illuminated the isle like magic. *Ka wehena o ke ao.* The opening of light. Gold and pink translucent light from the heavens danced upon blue-green verdant cliffs, from which plunged crystal riverlettes of shimmering water. The dissolving diaphanous morning mist over the land was lifting into the air, revealing incredibly cleaved gorges and plunging bluffs.

The silver mist is like the kapa of a beautiful woman, she thought, and she tilted her head to one side and smiled to herself. Yes, the morning is like a goddess releasing her silver robe. *Wehe a kohana.* Stripping naked. Perhaps to go bathe in the sea. Or to lie down with her lover.

And the rocking of the ship, up and down and side to side, so that everything was peculiarly out of focus, added to the illusion that the land before her was not truly real. A dreamland. Could any land be that lovely? Even the islands of her own native land were not this enchanting.

Her husband was by her side, talking to the white missionary Father, but she had no interest in what they were saying. She stood transfixed, looking out to sea, while her awareness was focused on the feeling running through the center of her body, flowing from her privates to between her eyes.

Are you an aumakua, a god? she thought, addressing this feeling inside her, for she had heard old stories of how ancestral spirits could take over the body, causing strange feelings and sensations, but quickly she remembered that the Father taught that were no such things as ancestral spirits. Gods did not reside in rocks and trees and sharks and owls. Turtles were just turtles; they could not teach one anything. Owls were just birds that hunted at night; they could not warn of danger or lead a lost one home. These things, birds and animals and stones, did not have souls. They were the One Almighty God's creations, but they could not go to the Great Heaven.

She felt instinctively, in her *opu*, though, in her belly, that there were such beings.

Now she found herself thinking about these things, which she knew she shouldn't. Thinking of the old ones, the gods and the ancestral spirits, was wrong. A sin. She knew this; still sometimes, she let herself dream of the old ways.

My mother's mother believed these things, she thought. My mother's mother's father fed the old ones, the gods. He burned sacrifices to them on altars of stone. Taro and banana. Black pig. Men. And the old ones, the gods, ate.

How could they eat, if, as the Father said, there were no such thing?

Pua'a he'a. Bloodstained pig. Human sacrifice, she mused. The worst sin, according to the missionary Father. It was good, according to the Father, to pretend sometimes

141

to eat the body of Jesus and to drink his blood, but... to really eat a man was an evil thing.

For some reason she almost felt like laughing, when she thought of eating Jesus. She tried to force her mind to think of only the One True God, but she couldn't.

Why, she wondered, was the one thing good and the other thing bad?

Once she had asked her husband to ask the Father about this, why they could pretend to eat Jesus, but it was the greatest sin to eat other men. The Father had then explained that the body of Jesus and the blood of Jesus were spirit and it was spirit that was absorbed during Communion.

But didn't spirit mean mana? she thought. And isn't that why her ancestors ate men?

Pua'a he'a, she thought. Bloodstained pig. Human sacrifice. The old ones and the old ways. She shuddered. But she also felt thrilled.

She gazed out over the waters. In her mind's eye, she saw many young girls swimming toward her, holding their kapas high over their heads as best they could with one hand. That was in the days of the kapus, when women and girls were not allowed even to touch canoes, she reflected. To touch a canoe would be death. And so the girls had swum to the ships.

My mother's mother swam to the great ships, she thought. She saw her, her mother's mother, in her mind's eye, climb dripping naked out of the sea, her long black hair shining and her brown breasts like coconuts, and offering herself shamelessly to the white men, believing they were men of great mana, even gods.

That was in the old times, when things were different, she thought. The days of pua'a he'a. Bloodstained pig. When men ate men and lovemaking was free, without sin.

Her husband touched her arm, and the feeling of excitement in her backbone vanished. She stared at him

142

for a moment as if she did not know who he was. He grinned at her amiably with very white, very healthy, shining teeth, and the coconut oil on his black hair, parted in the middle and combed like the missionary Father's, glistened in the sun. In one arm he held their sleeping child. It bothered her, she suddenly thought for the first time, that he combed his hair that way, like the Father's. But before she could think why, her thoughts were disrupted by a loud and confident voice, calling for Morning Prayer.

She turned reflexively toward the circle of men who stood with hands folded deferentially together and heads bowed to the floor of the ship. They were listening reverently while the Father, on one precariously balanced bended knee, thanked the Almighty God for bringing them safely to this benighted land, and then asked for the blessing of delivering these heathens unto the only True, Just, and Merciful Son of God.

These islanders are my cousins, she thought, and she felt that tingle of excitement beginning again, but then she remembered that these people were heathens. Heathens, she understood, were like animals. They looked like people, but acted like animals. They lived by the law of tooth and nail, the good Father had taught; they murdered one another and committed the vilest of sins—they ate one another.

The only difference between a heathen and an animal, a pig for example, or a dog, she knew, was that a heathen had a soul. And this soul was doomed to go to a fiery pit called Hell, for an eternal nighttime, to be tortured by a red devil, a terrifying creature like a giant cruel mo'o, a lizard as she envisioned it. Unless the heathen heard and accepted the Word of God.

The Father, the missionary and his wife and child, some natives who worked for the Mission, and a few armed sailors were deposited on shore, where the sullen

143

people stood looking at them suspiciously. The Father, chatting loudly, smiled kindly at them in a general way, and called out a greeting to them in their own language, which was much the same as her native tongue, but they returned his smile with hostile silent stares, which the Father seemed not to notice. The Father's natives busied themselves in gathering the boxes of supplies and personal belongings, while the sailors stood among them alert and wary. Her husband the missionary made himself very busy at something, avoiding confronting for a little while longer these scowling people, his distant brothers. Only she, holding her baby, stood quietly from where she had stepped onto the shore, and really looked back at the people.

They were fierce looking. The men, almost naked, were tattooed from the tops of their head to their feet, so that they seemed more bluish-black than brown. Some had long black hair, but shaved completely on one side of their heads, while some had completely hairless heads except for long black strands of hair fountaining from the very top of their skulls. They were tall, big men, with powerful bodies and fearless eyes. The women too, were large and potent looking, and the men and women were watching the disembarkment with mostly contemptuous disinterest from distrustful dark eyes. She had heard that these people, these islanders who were her distant cousins from centuries ago, were all descendants of ali'i, the chiefly class of her people. As she looked at them, she thought that this must be so. They were formidable and possessed mana, power.

How do I look to them? she wondered, as she stood and stared back at them with their same dark eyes, feeling self-conscious in the high-buttoned missionary dress and starched bonnet and leather shoes in which usually she took so much pride. She felt they were looking at her as if she were naked, as if she wore no clothes at all, but she didn't look away or down with a sense of modesty, as she was sure the missionary mothers would have done.

Yes, these brutal people were her cousins, separated by time and water. A fear pierced her, to think of being left alone here with just her husband and her child. The good Father and the white sailors and the natives from her own island would soon sail away and leave only the three of them, her husband to minister to these people and she to minister to her husband and child. The ship and the Father would not return until one year would pass.

They would not dare to harm us, she thought, not after what the French did to them. And the Spanish before that. They know they would be annihilated.

She continued to search the faces, one by one, fascinated by what she saw there, as if she were looking into a mirror for the first time, which, in a way, she was, until she was startled by the face of a woman that glared back at her with such sheer hatred that she almost dropped her baby. She herself stared back blankly, not understanding, until the huge bare-breasted woman turned abruptly and strode angrily away from the beach. Now she glanced at the man who had stood next to the angry giantess.

He too was huge, tall and almost naked. His black hair was tied into a knot at the back of his thick neck, and bluish-black lines in elaborate geometrical patterns were tattooed on one side of his face and down his muscular chest and arms.

Handsome as a hawk, she thought. He was looking back at her with such a look that now she did look down, and it was out of modesty. That feeling, that shiver of excitement, rose in her again. She glanced quickly at her husband, who was helping to unload a barrel, and then she looked again at the man.

To her amazement, there were two of them now, just alike. They both stood holding their arms daringly crossed

145

with their feet wide apart, and she saw they were boldly staring directly at her and laughing. Brothers, she thought. *Mahoe*. Twins. She had never seen twins before, though she had heard of them, and an ages-old primordial fear of whatever is strange, whatever is not customary, coursed through her body and made her feel defensive. Two of one kind, she thought. She held her baby closer and looked away.

The Father was calling her name and motioning for her and her husband to follow him through the glowering throng of islanders on the beach to the place where they would live. Her husband tripped nervously over a coiled bundle of rope as he hurried to the Father's side. Beads of sweat ran down his face.

Haoles, the white people, would never bring their women here, she thought, and she felt contempt for her husband, for the first time, for he had brought her here. Either he was a coward who dared not stand up to the missionary father and his teachings or he did not value her. She glanced at him with contempt. Her husband misread her look for fear and came to her and walked by her side through the people, who kept their distance but laughed scornfully.

"Think of Jesus," her husband whispered to her, and he smiled around amiably. But still the sweat was rolling from his brow.

The next days were busy days for all the men because the Father wanted to leave them as comfortable as possible, he said. He, her husband, and the mission natives built a stone house for them at the bottom of the forest not too far from the beach. She herself would have preferred a hale of pili grass, like the native huts, but the Father said that a stone house was better because it could not be burnt. She looked at him questioningly when he said this, but he merely smiled and walked away. She mostly sat with her baby and watched the men carry stones

146

and timber for this dark house that would soon be her new home. The ferocious-looking people came too and idled about and she watched them as they mockingly laughed at the stone house. Among those who came was the giantess she had seen when she had first disembarked. The woman stared at her until her angry eyes burned like coals. The mahoe sometimes came too and watched.

The Father walked briskly to and fro about his business, undaunted to pass among the people as he went back and forth from the ship, where the sailors, stripped to their waists because of the heat, still wore their guns.

After five days, the house was finished. That first evening in the stone house, she held her baby and looked into the fire while the Father and her husband and the ship's Captain talked of the ship's departure in the morning.

"Someday, Father, when we come, we must get up into the high forest to see those colossal ruins I told you about," said the Captain. "I should think you will find them very fascinating."

The Father replied, "I suppose they are ki'i, idols of their gods? Such as the Hawaiian islanders had years ago, before the temples were brought down and the hideous things burned?"

"I think not, Father," replied the Captain. "For one thing, they are colossal monuments carved in stone, rather than wood. Massive blocks of stone you must see to believe. How such blocks of stone could be transported up into the high forest is a mystery. And where did the stone come from? Where are the quarries? And some of them are toppled over, on their sides, or even upside down. Yet, not five-thousand men could move the largest of those stones. For another thing, even the natives here do not know who created them—they were here, according to them, long before their people first arrived. Gigantic carved stone heads with faces that are not of this world.

147

And cat-like creatures. The islanders, as you know, did not know of cats."

"They sound demonic," said the Father casually. "And how do the natives regard them?"

"They seem to believe they are supernatural," said the Captain. "Even the natives don't go up there much. *Ho'omanamana*, very superstitious of the place. Almost can't blame them myself."

The Father smiled. "That is what we are here for," he said. "To teach them the difference between superstition, and the Truth. To turn them from the way of the pagan, the path to hell, to the way of the Believer, the path to heaven." "Poor heathen souls," added the Father, and he smiled again.

"Yes, I heard today that they sacrificed and ate a six year old child just a month ago," the Captain said loudly and blithely, and then he snorted and his eyes laughed but he didn't even look in the direction of the woman holding the child. The Father did look at her, however, and the visage of concern he wore was quickly replaced with an exaggerated look of pity. He shook his head and spoke in a hushed voice of the horridness of the wicked crime.

"Let us pray," he said, and they all bowed their heads while black shadows danced like evil on the cold stone walls.

She lay awake long into the night, thinking with dread of tomorrow, and being left here alone. She thought of the conversation before the fire, and the sacrificed child.

"The most wicked sin," the Father had said. "To sacrifice a child."

Yet how is it, she wondered, that the One True God sacrificed his son, as the Holy Bible taught? She wanted to know these things.

In the morning, she, holding tight her sleeping child, and her husband, holding tight his Bible, stood on the beach and watched as the ship sailed away. The Father waved his hat merrily at them, as if he were off to a festivity, while she and her husband stared silently, until the Father was just a speck on the horizon. His last prayer, as he had knelt on the beach with his hat in his hand, had been about courage, and the will of God, and trust. His oiled head with its shiny bald spot had shone in the sunshine as he prayed on and on about service to the Almighty and humility toward the Supreme, while his eyelids closed tautly and his eyeballs danced jerkily when he turned his face up to heaven.

What does he see inside, that makes his eyeballs dance so? she had wondered, as she had looked down upon the old man kneeling in the sand. Does he see the One True God? Is God inside of him?

She turned from the disappearing speck on the sea toward her husband's face. The veins in his neck stood out and sweat rolled down his forehead, though the moist morning air was still cool. He felt her looking and turned toward her with the amiable, foolish smile, which he almost always wore now, except when they were alone, when he always looked worried, but she frowned slightly and indicated with her eyes the fierce people who had also gathered on the beach to watch the ship's departure. Now they were alone among them. As her husband, looking rigidly ahead, with his back very straight, led the way slowly up the beach, back to the stone house, she followed with small steps, wishing she could run, and she might have, if she had not been carrying the child.

*

The first days were filled with unspoken fear as she and her husband went about their everyday tasks. They were always being watched, spied upon. Some of the people would come and sit before the stone house and watch for entire mornings, to be replaced by people who

149

would come and sit and watch entire afternoons. Sometimes the giantess with the burning eyes of hatred came and sat before the house, watching malevolently. The twin men, the mahoe, often came and stood before the house. Sometimes only one came, and sometimes both. When both came, they would watch and laugh with one another.

Trying to be light-hearted, her husband said of the giantess, "I think she is jealous of your leather shoes."

She replied, "And those mahoe. They want your Bible."

"Those mahoe want you!" her husband said, and the remark was so unexpected and his tone so strange that she started.

"What do you mean?" she asked. And she was apprehensive of what he would say.

"Be careful. They are always watching you," he said. "And their woman. She is always watching you too."

"Their woman?" she repeated.

"Yes," he answered. "They are *punalua*. Sinful brothers who share one woman."

The first nights were the worst time. She and her husband with the sleeping child between them would lie silently on their mats in the dark, tense with listening. Between the sound of each wave of the sea, they strained to hear the crackling of murderous footsteps or the insidious murmur of voices. But they never talked about these things.

One night, though, sitting before the fire, she asked her husband if he believed in mana.

"Isn't it true," she asked, "the great King Kamehameha built a heiau to his god and offered human sacrifice, and he won a kingdom? Surely he acquired mana from his offering to his god."

"It seems true," her husband answered. "But those who make offerings to the devil, reap evil. Though the

150

King won a kingdom, much blood was shed; lives were lost. In truth, the King reaped evil."

She reflected on this for a time.

"Then why," she asked, "did the One True God sacrifice his only son? What did he reap?"

Her husband reflected for a moment. "He won our souls," answered her husband, "for all who believe on Jesus have everlasting life and will sit on the right hand of the throne of God."

"And why does the One God want our souls?" she asked, for she really wished to understand these things.

"Because souls are most precious," her husband answered. He paused. "Because God is love." He looked at his wife sadly, when he said the word love.

She said nothing to this. Clearly, though, she thought, there was mana in sacrifice.

She and her husband began to prefer to remain inside the dark stone house, even during most of the day, though neither of them spoke it. Hiding like little crabs, she thought. Her husband would sit inside for hours and read his Bible, preparing his first sermon for the people, he said. She sat still against the wall, holding the child, and watched his lips move as he leaned over the pages with tense concentration, resting his forehead in his hands, until she reminded him that they needed water. He would open the door and stare out up into the forest so long she would become stiff with apprehension. At last, he would turn to say something to her, and his face looked agonized, but the words wouldn't come, and finally he would turn and just go.

"When will the man of God preach to the people?" she asked him one day, and she began to taunt him, and he taunted her in return, for their nerves were on edge.

"And when will you befriend the women?" he asked. "When will you show them the loom?"

"When you become the man, I will become the woman," she replied aggressively.

One morning she went to the stream and fetched the water herself. She carried her child on her hip as she climbed up the forest trail to the stream. She could feel she was being watched. She laid the child in the grass and waded into the stream and let the soothing water flow over her legs. Her body responded to the sunlight and the forest and the water just as it had when she had been a child on her own island, not so many years ago.

Why did I come here? she thought. She glanced at her child. Why do I have this child? she wondered. Then she felt guilty, for hadn't the missionary mother taught her that her godly role was to be a helpmate and a mother?

Her mother and father had sent her to the missionary school, and her husband's mother had sent him. They had learned not just their letters and numbers but most importantly, they had learned about Jesus and the father of Jesus who is God and about sin and about redemption. They had learned about Eternal Life. They had easily believed everything they had been taught, though they did not always understand. Nevertheless, it was the good Father and the missionary Mother who told them they should marry one another and witness for Jesus to the heathen. Having been always obedient, this they had done.

Now she was here. Suddenly, she didn't wish to think of it anymore. She was tired of anxiety and fear.

She listened to the sweet songs of the forest birds and threw off the terrible suspense of the past days. She no longer cared if someone were watching her. She tossed her dress aside and lay down in the shallow sun-warmed water and let the tension in her body dissolve in the sunlight. She lay there a long, long time, at last even closing her eyes and almost drifting into sleep. Her child's cry startled her and she sat up abruptly. She waded from the stream and picked up the child. Hearing something on the other side of the stream, she turned to look. One of the mahoe had been watching.

When she returned to the stone house, her husband was furious to know she had lain naked in the stream. Why she told him, she didn't understand. She in turn taunted him about his first sermon, and he hurled his Bible at her. She laughed at him, and called him a coward. He began shouting.

From outside came the sound of two voices laughing. She walked outside and saw the mahoe, who stood for a moment staring and laughing and then turned their backs to her and walked away.

From that time, she knew she did not love her husband. She slept next to him on the mat, but it was like sleeping with a distasteful stranger. The smell of his breath angered her.

One day soon after this he told her he was ready to preach his first sermon to the people.

"Under the trees," he said. "Tomorrow at the time of great mana, at noontime. When my shadow shall enter my head."

They quarreled because she did not want to go, but he insisted. Wasn't she his wife, his helpmate?

She stood behind him in the shade of the trees while the people, curious, gathered on the beach in response to his call, and he began to speak of the old ways, and how the old ways were wrong, and he told about sin, and the evil of sacrificing and eating men, and how sin could be washed white as snow. The mahoe were there; they didn't seem to be listening; they were watching her. The giantess, the woman of the mahoe, was there too, staring with hatred. Sweat dripped from her husband's brow, and when he tried to smile compassionately, as the Father would have done, if the Father had been here, his face looked contorted and not human. Like a gasping fish, she

153

thought.   In the beginning, the people laughed, some children threw stones, and then they drifted away, a few at a time, until no one else was listening. She followed him wordlessly to the stone house where he sat and sobbed.

At first, she felt sorry for him, to see him sob so, but when he insisted he wept for the people, for their evil and ignorant ways, she felt contempt. She sat against the cool stones in the dark of the house and watched him. At the sound of a thud against the house, he rose and walked outside.   She followed.   Her husband stood holding something like a stick, and when she put out her hand to take it, it was the hollow section of a human leg bone. One of the mahoe stood against a coconut tree, watching them with amused eyes.

After the sermon, she and her husband rarely spoke. She began to take long walks down the beach, carrying the child on her hip, stooping to collect mollusks. Sometimes she sat and watched the waves, while the child played on the sand. Often she watched the women go into the sea naked. Sometimes, in the evening, she watched the men in their canoes, gliding onto shore in the last golden light of the sun. One day she watched one of the mahoe ride the wild waves to shore right to where she was sitting. She grabbed up the child and hurried away.

Then she began to go for long walks on the beach at night, leaving the child in the stone house with its father. Her husband protested, but still she would go. Once, on the night of the full moon, she came upon a girl and a boy making love on the sand. They hadn't heard her, and she stood quietly in the shadows and listened to their love sounds. The strange and pleasant feeling that she hadn't felt in so long ran up her spine.

When she returned to the stone house, her husband was sitting before a candle, doing nothing. He stared at her ominously, and then he tried to smile in a friendly way, but she said nothing to him and lay down on the mat in the

154

dark. She wished he would go away. She lay and remembered the lovers on the beach. She imagined that she were the girl, and what it would be like to make love at night in the sand under the moon. She knew she should not be thinking these things, but she could not help herself.

Her husband coughed, so that she grimaced to herself, but then she forgot him and went back to her reverie. She thought about her mother and father, and tried to imagine how it must have been, how they must have made love, when she was made. She imagined the long line of kanaka before her, people who had made her. The long line of her ancestors making passionate love. To make her.

Not all people make love the same, she thought. She remembered stories her mother's mother had told her, when she was just a girl, stories of the old days, of how girls, in the old times, were taught the art of love. And *hana aloha*. Love sorcery.

Her husband came and lay beside her, breathing in her hair, so that she turned her back to him.

"Why do you turn your back to me? I am not a dog," he whispered, but she pretended to be already asleep. She thought about the mahoe. She wondered if mahoe, twins, made love the same. She wondered if these mahoe pleased their woman, the giantess, the same way. Then she wondered if she were pleasing to them; she knew she was. When she heard that her husband was sleeping, she touched her own thighs.

One day she left the child with her husband and climbed up into the forest further than she had ever climbed. She stopped by a stream for water, and when she looked up, both mahoe stood just steps from her. One made a silent motion for her to follow, and she did. And that is how she came to leave her husband and child.

High, high up they climbed, the three of them silent, as in a dream. They led her to their hale pila, which was surrounded by a neat and fertile wetland taro patch. She entered the hale, following them, and knew immediately that a woman had been living there. As in a silent dream, she lay down on the tapa mat and became the woman of the mahoe.

As in the kapu days of her own people, the men did the cooking. She weeded the taro patch and swept the hale, but other that that, there was not much for her to do. The mahoe were often absent the entire day, or sometimes several days. But even when they were there, it was a silent household, for the mahoe talked together in low tones, if at all, for they had not much need to talk, being the same. To her they talked not at all, and never smiled, but she liked the way they held her, when they lay on the mat.

She began to amble about the forest, sometimes spending whole days beside a stream, just sitting and watching the water. Sometimes she felt uneasy, she felt that the jungle had eyes that were watching her; she knew this could not be—she and the two men were completely alone, for no one else came up here.

When some weeks had passed, she decided to walk the forest trail down to the village—she would hide in the trees and watch her husband and child, for she was curious how their lives were going without her, though it cannot be said she longed for them. Before she was halfway down, however, one of the mahoe, who had been trailing her, beat her so badly she thought she would die. After that, she dared not go down the trail. Now she knew she could never return to her husband; the mahoe would most certainly kill her, and perhaps her husband and child. She confined her wanderings to the upper forests.

More time passed, and she knew she had conceived a child. Her belly grew big. One day, while the mahoe were away, she ate some black pig that the mahoe had offered to their gods. Such food was kapu for the native women of this island, as it had been once for her own ancestors, but she licked her greasy fingers with relish.

Perhaps it was the eating of the kapu pig that had been offered to the heathen gods—for what is reaped is what is sown—but great darkness entered her life thereafter. When the mahoe returned, and found that she had eaten the forbidden food, she was beaten until she lost the child. After this, she was beaten more and more often, for no reason at all, until her legs and arms always showed fresh or fading blue marks. At first, she protested these beatings, and tried to fight back, but she soon learned it was better to just crouch like an animal silently on the ground and let them strike her until they stopped.

*

A year passed, and the ship carrying the good father sailed confidently into the bay. When the Father found out the state of things, and heard the story, alone—or so he thought, for the eyes of one mahoe were following him— he climbed the trail to the jungle hale, intent on persuading the missionary's wife to return to her husband, child, and Christian duties. Intrepidly, for he knew the mahoe would dare not harm him, he entered the hale where she was seated on the mat with one of the mahoe; the other entered stealthily behind him. The good Father removed his hat and sat on the mat before the woman with the big belly, for she had conceived once again. He noted the bruises on her face immediately.

Silently, looking down, she listened while the Father first implored her in the name of God, duty, and motherhood, to return to her husband. She looked up only once, not at the father, but at the mahoe, who stared at her ominously, and then looked at one another, grinning. She looked down at the ground again, dark and silent. The good Father next commanded her, in the name of God, duty, and motherhood, to return with him. He stood to his feet, and held his hand out to her, expecting her to obey and go with him, but she remained where she was, silent and motionless. Once more, he commanded, and then he begged her, in the name of Almighty God, to please return with him, but she only drew her legs up in her arms, as if she were crouching, as if she were making herself as small as possible, as if she were being beaten, and still she was silent.

"If you decide to return to civilization," said the Father, and he looked around the hut contemptuously, "there will be ships coming in now every few weeks. You can return to your island. Tell the captain I will pay your fare." Then the good Father shook his head, upon which he replaced his hat, and said, "May God help you," and with one last pitiful look at her, he departed.

The missionary husband, downcast and ashamed, was nevertheless waiting with a hopeful heart for the return of the Father and his wayward wife. When he saw the Father return alone, his shame before the men, the Father, the Captain, the soldiers, knew no bounds. The Father, sensitive to the man's mortification, projected an attitude of buoyant optimism.

"Sooner or later she will return," he said convincingly. However, he could not bring himself to tell the husband the condition of his wife—the bruises, the despondency, the big belly.

"I believe," said the good Father, when he related everything to the Captain, "that she is being intimidated. She looks very ill used, and is covered with bruises. With the aid of the soldiers, I believe we could force her return."

But the Captain and the soldiers were reluctant to risk injury, or their lives, for the sake of a run-away errant woman. After all, they said, she was just a native. They refused to become involved.

When the good Father departed, ten days later, he admonished the husband to keep the faith, pray without ceasing, do his Heavenly Father's work with zeal, and he reminded him that victory would be God Almighty's. He himself and the ship would return in another year, and by that time, undoubtedly, the misguided wife would have returned, and should be received with forgiveness and mercy. And so once again, the missionary stood on the beach, holding his little son's hand, and watched the Father wave merrily, as the ship disappeared over the horizon.

One day, as the woman rambled about the forest, she was sure she heard something behind her. She stopped to listen, thinking that perhaps a wild pig was following her, for wild boars were dangerous, and even more so, the wild sows. She heard nothing, and continued on to her favorite place by a stream. Again, she thought she heard footsteps, and again she stopped to listen; she thought she had heard human footsteps. Again, she heard nothing. Reaching the stream, she waded across as fast as she could, for she was greatly encumbered by the child she carried in her belly. She hid behind a bush for a very long time, watching, but at last, seeing and hearing nothing, she rose. Whatever had been following her was gone. She wandered on. She had never been on this side of the stream, and when she saw what seemed a path, though greatly overgrown, she followed it.

Dully curious to know where this path led, she climbed upward and upward, sometimes losing the path, until she untangled the vines and branches of the dense growth and found it again. She wandered as if in a dream. This was her life now, wandering about in the forest, sometimes working the taro, eating and sleeping with the mahoe at night—her old life had faded away, as if it had been a dream of no significance—her husband, her child, she felt no connection to them any longer. One night and day folded into another, all alike. Nothing she had learned in the mission school mattered here. The good Father no longer mattered; the missionary mother no longer mattered. The past had no importance, no relevance. Her entire past seemed unreal; in fact, her entire life seemed only a continuous illusory dream.

At one point, attempting to penetrate a particularly dark and dense area of fern growth, she stooped to examine the path and realized that actually she was walking on a sort of wall. She looked up. What she saw sent a great shiver up her backbone.

Huge menacing figures with horrible features stared back at her. Instinctively she knew—this was a place of mana. This was a place of kapu.

There before her were great inhuman faces with extraordinary expressions that struck terror into her heart. Enormous monuments, some half-buried, of strange, melancholy figures—unfamiliar, inhuman—tumbled about, covered in moss and ferns. Animals—fishes, birds, turtles—carved in gigantic black boulders, seemed alive and threatening, as if they were floating and flying through the gloom. She would have fled but she was riveted by fear. She stood in the damp shadows, trembling with fright.

These are the ki'i of which the Captain spoke, she thought. She squatted on the soggy ground, for her legs felt weak as if they wouldn't hold her. Yes, most certainly, this was a place of mana. For a long time she squatted and stared, crouched like an animal. Her eyes rested most often on one colossal figure, the top of upon which was carved a long smooth platform, which in fact was an altar.

*

A few weeks later, when the birth pains began, she left the hale of the mahoe and disappeared into the jungle, as was the native custom, for the defiling blood of

160

childbirth was kapu. Carrying a calabash of poi and a calabash of water, she laboriously climbed the path to the place of mana. She felt the eyes of the jungle upon her. She stopped and looked back several times to see if someone were following, but when she stopped, she heard nothing but the calls of the forest birds.

Painstakingly, by climbing upon large boulders that seemed to serve as gigantic steps, she scaled the most hideous of the idols, the one upon which was carved the long smooth platform. At the very top, by leaning over the stone on her belly, she was able to hoist herself with difficulty upon the mossy surface of the cold stone. She then lay and rested in the cool shadows.

Within a few hours, she had delivered the baby. The tiny child screamed furiously but here in the dank, earthy jungle, in the midst of the huge mossy boulders, the cries were muffled. She cut the umbilical cord, and placed the child beside her.

She stared at it. Its crinkled face resembled the catlike creatures carved in the great stones around her. She lifted her calabash and took a drink of cool water. It tasted good. She dipped her finger in the water and then placed it on the screaming child's lips. Reflexively the child stopped screaming and began to suckle her finger. She removed her finger and, in a moment, the child began screaming again. She watched it with dispassion.

Yes, I have become a heathen, she thought. I do not feel love inside; I do not feel God inside.

She sat on the stone for many hours, gathering her strength, staring at the howling, crinkled-faced baby lying in the moss. At last, the angry-faced newborn ceased crying, and lay absolutely still. She gathered her calabashes, tied them to her back, and stood to her feet. She stared down at the baby lying in the moss. Rain began to fall. Hadn't rain always been a sign of blessing since time began? Large raindrops fell upon the baby's face, and the baby made a weak movement, as if it made one last attempt to suckle.

She stooped at the edge of the stone. She turned and lay full length on her belly on the mossy stone platform, searching with her foot for the boulder below her upon which she could step and descend. A slight sound and movement against her foot startled her and she quickly turned her head to look back upon a face so intent on evil it could have only come from Hell, but she was powerless to protect herself against the giantess who sprang upon her with fury and stabbed her through the heart.

The warm jungle raindrops fell upon her as she lay sprawled on her belly upon the cold mossy stone, the little baby just a step away; in the gathering gloom as the day slipped into night, the night birds began to woo one another.

*

Ever true to his word, the good Father, in the confident little ship, sailed again into the harbor. He was busy with many tasks, one of which was once again to climb the jungle path, to the hale of the mahoe, to persuade the missionary's wife to return. This time, in a show of authority, he took two soldiers with him. The mahoe were there, and stood and looked at him contemptuously.

"Where is the woman?" the good Father demanded in their language.

They seemed surprised, and looked at one another, for they had thought the woman had returned to her island in one of the ships that had sailed into the harbor. They stared at him silently. One of them pointed to the taro patch. The giantess, who had been squatting in the field, rose to her full height. She glared scornfully.

The good Father paused for a moment, resting both hands upon his walking stick, and then he and the soldiers turned and departed.

That night, around the fire in the stone house, the Captain and the good Father spoke in low tones, for the missionary and his little son had gone to bed.

"Yes, the mahoe have murdered her," said the good Father, and he shook his head sadly. "Probably beaten to death. The former wife, the giantess, is reinstated, it seems." He exhaled noisily and made a pitiful face. "I do feel somewhat responsible."

The Captain smiled. "She did what she wanted," he said.

"Yes," said the Father, "but I did bring her here." He sighed.

"God has given us all free choice," said the Captain, in an ironic tone, for the Captain was not much of a believer. "Isn't that what the Good Book says?"

The good Father did not hear the irony and seemed comforted. "Yes, that is true," he said.

The Captain nodded toward the sleeping missionary. "And him?" he asked.

"He and the child will return with us," said the Father. "Two years, and not one soul won for God." And the Father shook his head disapprovingly, rose, stirred the ashes, and went to bed.

*

The day before the departure, the Captain and the good Father made the arduous climb upward into the jungle to the place of the ki'i.

"Good God!" exclaimed the Father when he saw the hideous monuments. "What testament to evil!"

163

The Captain grinned, and began scampering among the ruins. The Father followed more carefully. They scrambled about silently for a time exploring the enormous, mossy, black stones. All was still except for the eerie calls of jungle birds.

"Up here!" called the Captain, who stood upon the long smooth platform of the largest of the sinister monuments.

The good Father climbed warily upon boulder steps to the top of the monument and hoisted himself to where the Captain squatted, pointing to something in the moss. It was a femur bone.

"*Iwi hilo*," said the good Father. "Human. A thighbone."

The Captain turned the bone over in the moss. The underside was white as snow. "You know," said the Captain, "the natives cherish the bones of the dead; they believe that the soul is connected to the bones. That is why they are always so careful to hide the bones of their dead."

"Poor savages," said the Father, compassionately, but he wore a look of contempt. "They shall burn in Hell forever." He looked all around with revulsion.

"There are some," said the Captain, audaciously, with a twinkle in his eye, "who think that things are what you believe them to be. Heaven is what you believe it to be, and so is Hell."

"Is that right?" said the Father, with a satiric smile.

"Yes," said the Captain. He picked up the bone and examined it for a moment, turning it right and left.

"I believe it came from a woman," said the Captain.

"How can you tell?" asked the good Father.

"Just a feeling," said the Captain.

The good Father said nothing, but smirked.

164

"Just think," said the Captain, without looking at the good Father, "of all the times this thighbone, this... how did you call it?"

"Iwi hilo," said the good Father.

"Just think," said the Captain, "of all the times this iwi hilo once grinded and thrashed about in the dark."

He glanced at the good Father. The good Father looked shocked.

The Captain chuckled, wet the tip of his finger with his saliva, and very, very slowly traced the underside of the bone, which was as white as snow, from one end to the other. He looked up at the good Father and smiled broadly, then tossed the bone, white as snow, out into the moss-covered stones, where no one would ever disturb it again.

THE BIRTHING STONES

They came with the first migrators hundreds even thousands of years ago, some say long before the birth of *Dia Chrstou o Goistais*, Christ the magician, who walked on water and brought the dead to life again and turned water into wine, for didn't Christ know that this world is not what it appears to be?

Wrapped in dried sea grasses, cradled in leaves and secured in a dried gourd, they sailed across the sea for days upon days, rocked like an unborn baby snuggled in warm womb waters. They could feel they were a long way from where they were born, their home, but they were not afraid, for there is only one thing they were afraid of, and that was being shattered into pieces or rent apart or split in two. Dissolving away over eons is not so much a death as a slow and peaceful resurrection into pearls, which was the most auspicious fate of their kind, and what they longed for. Very very rare it was that one died violently.

So they sailed in their little ark for days, neither bored nor agitated but dully curious. By day they could sense the vibration of the muffled voices of busy bodies, which was their way of hearing. By day, they could feel the searing hot presence of the sun, even though they rested securely in their dark hold, and by the same token, at night they could feel the stars swirling above them as they drifted toward Hokule'a, the star of joy, lulled by the sleepy rhythm of the deep.

166

On several occasions, however, they were thrown violently about. The roaring of thunder and the pitching and falling and crashing of their little ark against the sides of the larger vessel for days on end made them homesick rather than seasick, for they missed the splash and rhythm and rolling of the surf and the spray of water on their obdurate skins, but later, when they heard screams and moans of fear from the terrified women, they had the first sinking slow dread that even they might be broken into bits, shattered, and flung onto the bottom of the seafloor. And once, on a still night when the great double-hulled canoe sat as motionless in the doldrums as a fishing heron waiting to ambush its prey, feeling the pull of the full moon, that Queen of the Night, they felt so lonely and inconsolable they would have cried, if they could have made tears.

But they could not make tears, because they were stones. All they could do was wait. Waiting was their strength, indeed, their life.

They could wait a long long time, for stones have a long long history of just listening and patiently waiting, not ever really expecting anything to happen, but even they became hopeful and thrilled when they heard the excited and happy shouts of the voyagers; they knew something different was happening. The people scurried about and then there was a thud, and then a cry of joy in unison from the people who had been so long hungry and thirsty at sea, and after a few minutes, the double-hulled canoe was quiet and definitely lighter. It bobbed up and down like a dry coconut, and the sounds of the disembarked people came from far away.

They waited and waited more days and nights (what else could they do?) thinking that perhaps they were forgotten after all, when finally, the little ark they rested in was lifted and carried a distance, then the gourd was opened, the leaves parted and the grasses unwrapped and bright light streamed into their awareness. They felt the always-alien living touch of human fingers, as strange to them as is the touch of centipede skin to humans, and the next thing they knew, they were held high in two oily palms as an oblation to the sunlight. Then the two palms slipped them down down onto the sand, and there they lay, free again at last, one with the other, the male with the female.

They had traveled thousands of miles across the open ocean, and now, like the *pua'a*, *moa* and *'īlio*, were set free. To propagate, to make more, to increase. Male and female, they were blessed by the people to go forth and multiply, to cover the island. But unlike the pig, the chicken and the dog, the little stones were not brought by the people to be eaten. They were not brought to be used as tools like the adze and they were not brought to be ornaments like the whalebone.

They were brought to remind the people that reality is not fixed. They were brought to remind the people that the world is not what we think it is. They were brought to remind the people that there are no limits. They were brought to remind the people that things are not what they seem—the greenness of grass is not really the green we think it is, the hardness of stones is not what we think it is, and even the crystal liquidity of water is not what we think it is. In short, they were brought because they were magic.

They were birthing stones, magic pebbles— *'ili'ili hanau.*

The little stones, the 'ili'ili hanau, saw right away that they were not the first stones on the beach, though they were by far the smallest. They looked around and saw that it was all good, and like home. Here too were all the same stones of their homeland. Much larger stones, some so large a man could sit on them, so large that it took two men or more to carry them, were here. And there were others that ranged in size from these larger stones to stones not much larger than they themselves. These stones possessed their own powers. But magic like theirs? No.

There was the *pohaku o Kane*, the stone that sent dreams to the people on behalf of the god Kane, and offered them forgiveness when they had done wrong, and inspiration to make things *pono*, right. In return, the people made offerings of pig and *kava* and *tapa* cloth, and planted the green *ti* and ferns around the altar stone, which delighted Kane. Then there were the *kuula* stone, the fisherman's stone, which stood near the shore and attracted the fish with its mana. There were stones possessed by *'aumakua* gods, which granted certain favors to those who worshipped them, like protection if one should become lost in the mighty *koa* forests. And there were great stones, cool and smooth, on which the regal princesses labored as they gave birth, surrounded by silent, unsmiling sentinels of chiefs and royal retainers. There were fertility stones shaped like the privates of a man, to which the young *wahine* prayed, hopeful of becoming *hapai*, with child.

Then there were stones important for their usefulness. There was the *pohaku anai pua'a,* the stone for rubbing off the singed hair of the pig. There was the stone used for the anchor of the canoe, and the stone used for the octopus lure, *naninui.* There was the stone used to sharpen tools, the rolling millstone, and the stone made into the hammer. There was the *poi* pounder and the stone used for the foundation of the sleeping and eating *hale.* There was the stone meant for rubbing the back when it ached. There was the *pohaku ho'oikaika,* its weight used for training the arms and legs big and strong for war, and there was the stone canoe breaker which men hurled with fury into the canoes of other men, breaking them into splinters, and then rolling it back again by ropes, to be cast out with fury again if luck was with them. There was the stone hammer used under water to break the enemy canoe into bits, the

169

pohaku waiki, and there was the stone used to split the breadfruit. There was the *pohaku kikeke*, the stone gong, which called the people to come gather together, and there was the stone used to divide one chief's land from the other, to keep the peace, the *ahu*.

But as practical and useful as stones might be for the people, and as much mana as they might possess, their magic did not approach that of the ʻiliʻili hanau, as you shall see.

While the people set about doing their work, making their homes, planting their crops, fishing and hunting, the little stones sat in their newly assigned place high up on the beach, away from the tide, for generally stones do remain in place if they are not disturbed. They themselves would have liked to roll and toss with the sea foam, but the people were afraid they might become lost in the surf. And as yet, there only the two of them, the male and the female.

Finally, one day, a child went running to the people, crying, "The ʻiliʻili hanau —they have made one baby!"

The people dropped their work and ran to see. And there it was, a little black and gray mottled pebble, smooth as a reed grass, sitting snug between the two larger pebbles. The people passed the baby stone around, hand to hand, and marveled at the miraculous—that the green of grass is not what we think it is, that the crystal liquidity of water is not what we think it is, that stones can give birth, that life is not what we think it is—but in the end, they placed the baby—a male pebble, for he was as smooth as smooth can be—back next to his parents, his mother and his father.

And it happened that another day, another child came running and said, "The ʻiliʻili hanau have made one baby again."

And the people ran again, and admired the new offspring, and worshipped the miraculous, the magic of existence. And they placed the baby—a girl this time, for she was not smooth but pitted—back with her parents and her brother, and now there were four stones.

In this way, the stones multiplied, and the people's faith in magic was sustained, for what is more unrealistic than a stone that can give birth? They continued to believe that at night one's spirit left through the tear duct of the eye, and that one could make wishes in dreams that would come true. They knew that dreaming of losing a tooth foretold the death of a family member. They knew that gods dwelled in plants and animals, in the water, in the sky, in the rocks, in the wind, in the flames of the volcano, and that these gods could be offended and placated. There is more to the world than meets the eye!

And after many years, the 'ili'ili hanau stretched up and down the beach as far as a human eyeball could see. While the other stones, mana such as they possessed, still sat single and barren, two by two the little stones had multiplied—brown ones, black ones, white ones, golden colored ones, spotted —the smooth males and the pitted females. Now they were free to roll and play in the tide. At low tide they sat quietly in place, silent witnesses to the sun, the wind, the clouds, as did the bigger stones. They sat quietly and listened to the people, who were ever busy, doing this and that.

At high tide, however, the stones were not at all silent. The waves of the sea would come, and the 'ili'ili hanau would roll up and down in the surf and toss and turn with the white-headed foam, and then their song could be heard up and down the beach for a great distance— clattering, chattering, gossiping, singing and laughing.

What did they sing of?

Their memories, for stones have very long memories. They remember forever; as long as they exist, as long as even their particles exist, they remember. Stones all over

171

the world have this memory, stretching back to the beginning of time. They are keepers of time and memory.

But when, after many years they had multiplied so profusely, some were gathered by the people and used to build walkways, and sometimes the busy people built great *heiau,* temples, using the large stones, and filled in the crevices with some of the 'ili'ili hanau. There to the dismay of the little stones, sticky red man blood flowed over the little stones, but the stones could not cry out with alarm. At other times, the people sang and, drunkenly picking up the stones, clacking them together, made music and danced ecstatically. The busy people buried the *iwi,* the bones of their own nearby in the grasses, and outlined their graves with the little stones, which made the little stones laugh, for they knew that long after the bones had disintegrated, they, the stones, would still be there.

And then something completely unexpected happened. These people who believed in magic, who had brought their magic with them over thousands of miles of open sea—they disappeared.

The heiaus no longer ran with blood, the people no longer cared for the iwi, the bones of their dead. The stone fishing god stood silent and unattended. The royal princesses never groaned in pain on the great stones again. The *pohaku o Kane,* the altar of that great god, stood unadorned. Only one man and his family remained. One man who understood the magic, and taught his children about the magic. A *hoa 'aina,* a caretaker, who understood the silence of the stones at low tide and their song when the waves washed high.

Na Huihui o Makali'i, those seven stars famed to all peoples, passed overhead again and again, the son of the caretaker became the new caretaker, and his son after him, but the day came when the caretaker disappeared. The 'ili'ili hanau dully wondered what had happened, but for the most part, they were just as pleased to be left alone, and at first, quietly continued to multiply.

But then the nightmare began.

People appeared who were not at all like those who believed in magic. To these people, the grass was green, water merely water, and a stone was a stone. They would come with big sacks and fill the bags to the brim with the little stones, and the kinfolk of the stones would be hauled away, never to be seen again. At first the little stones dully wondered what had happened to their kinfolk, but when big bare patches began to appear on their beach, they became disturbed. They were relieved when, after 20 years of being plundered, a caretaker appeared once again, one who believed in the magic.

*

Kapono sat, with the gods' permission, on the largest of all the stones on the beach, the birthing stone of kings, with one elbow resting on his knee, and his head resting on his hand, looking just like Rodin's Le Penseur, except that he did not appear to be a large, heroic figure. Rather, he was a small, wiry man, with miniature, tight muscles in his arms and calves, with small, splayed feet and long stringy hair, balding at the top, and there was a certain pathos about him. Kapono had the wise, weathered look of a sage of the Orient, like a Confucius, or a Lao Tzu, but he also looked tired, defeated. He was not naked either, but wore an old pair of cutoffs, so that he looked like a hungry castaway, or a homeless person. Like Le Penseur, however, his back rippled with tensed muscles, and his face was lost in thought.

He was considering paradise, and like Dante, he believed he was about to enter the gates of Hell.

Of course, Kapono had never heard of Dante.

173

Soon they would come for him. The authorities. The police with their eviction papers. The media. Probably the mayor's representative. The mayor would unlikely come again, as he was a busy man (no more shaka shaka and bradda bradda). The county officials would circle round him, like a false *lei* of sorrow, all wearing their nicest Aloha shirts, since they figured they would be on the evening news, and one of them would read from his expensive black leather notebook the final eviction notice: Kapono must leave immediately, his family's ancient land was being set aside as "land for all, for a park, a conservation area." They would all talk softly and compassionately, as if they really cared that a man was losing his home. That a land was losing its caretaker. That the places where rested the bones of the ancestors would become tourist attractions; indeed, the bones themselves might be stored in dusty cardboard boxes stacked in some museum, or even worse, in some truck on a construction site. That the gentle and placid green *honu*, asleep in her shell in the hot sand, would be terrified by the screams of undisciplined squads of children throwing rocks at her.

That the little stones, the *'ili'ili hanau* would become barren, would never give birth again.

That reality would become fixed.

That magic would vanish.

Of course, the real truth was not that the land was being set aside for a park, or a conservation area. Or "for all." The land would eventually be traded to some hotel developer for a cool one hundred million, a golf course for celebrities would be built, and who knows what would become of the magic.

When they had first come, just three years ago, the people from the county, he had welcomed them and spent a whole morning talking story and smiling and laughing with them, just as he used to do with most of those who ventured all the way down to his hut by the sea. He had

174

not really understood what their black notebooks and measuring tapes and hand-held calculators had meant. When they had talked about a custodian of the land, he had thought they meant him. He was pleased at this, but he quickly made it clear that it was his duty, his life purpose. He was the *kahu* of the *'aina*, the caretaker of the land, just as his father had been, and his father before that. When one man, who was from the Office of Native Affairs had mentioned that there might be some kind of money in it for him, some kind of stipend, he had assured them that he had no need of money.

They had looked coyly at one another and smiled, and he had thought at the time even that there was something sinister about their smiles.

"I have everything," he had said, not boastfully but proudly, disregarding their smiles. He had turned toward the sparkling blue-green sea with its frothy whitecaps and made a generous motion with his arms, and in his mind, with his sweeping gesture he had said it all. He was indeed the luckiest of men alive. And didn't the sea return his gesture with a great rush of her own huge white arms?

"I was born here," he said. "Right over here, on the lava, is my *piko*."

Walking lithely as a goat, while they clumsily followed, crunching the stones with their heavy shoes, Kapono led them over to a smooth stretch of lava a bit higher than the rest of the beach.

"And there's my father's piko and my father's father's piko," he said, pointing at little indentations in the lava.

"What's a piko?" one *haole* man, wearing shiny leather shoes and a big gold watch whispered audibly to another man.

"Piko is the umbilical cord," the man from the Office of Native Affairs answered. "In the old days they used to bury them because they believed it kept the family intact."

"Say, what's this?"

175

One man pointed to a carving in the rock, a stick figure with something like a bow stretching over his shoulder.

"That one's called 'Anuenue Man'," said the man who was the expert on native affairs. "Rainbow man."

"What's the meaning?" the first man said, and looked up at Kapono.

"That's me," said Kapono, and he changed the subject by making the sweeping gesture toward the land and sea again, for there were some things too sacred to talk about. And didn't the sea return his gesture with a great sweep of her own white arms?

"I have no need of money," he had told them. "There is nothing here that the *'aina*, this sacred land, does not give me. Look! With coconut fronds I have made my *hale*, I drink the sacred water from the underwater springs, just as my fathers have, my food is given to me from the sea. The sun and the moon and the stars are my best friends. I have everything."

"Yes," he said, "I am fortunate. *Ku ka hale I Punalu'u, i Ka-wai-hu-o-Kauila.* I am he who has found peace and comfort at last."

Because he loved to talk story, he began the story of the honu *Kauila*, the mythical sea turtle, whose parents dug her a fresh water pond, and who, when she became grown, developed a fondness for the children who came sometimes and played at the pond. In fact, she sometimes transformed herself into a little girl in order to play with them.

"It was Kauila who gave fresh water to the people here. It was she who created the fresh water springs where we have dived to collect the water in gourds for hundreds of years. There's her pond, right over there. Yes, I am very fortunate."

One haole man said, "That's real nice how you tell the story. You would make a great tourist guide."

176

He glanced over at the other men in such a way that Kapono felt the man had not meant it as a compliment at all.

"What about when you go to town?" one big haole man with a fat gut had asked him, and he had frowned down at Kapono's dirty feet. "Don't you need shoes?"

Kapono pointed to his bony, splayed feet. "I have Hawaiian feet," he said. "I do not need shoes."

The men had smiled politely and looked at one another with twinkles in their eyes, like they knew a good joke, a fact that he had noticed and put away in his mind to think about later, for their smiles definitely made him a bit uneasy, but he did not know why.

"What about when it comes time to pay taxes?" the big haole asked bluntly. "You must get a pretty hefty tax bill every year, huh?" He cast his evil eyes around, taking in the sea, the land, the mountains. "Yeah, a couple miles of shore-front prime ocean property. Wonder how much the taxes are?"

"This is sacred land," said Kapono. "It is not taxed."

The visitors all laughed. One said, "You wish!" Another said, "Everything is taxed. You know what they say, two things you have to do—pay taxes and die!" A third man murmured, "You can't squeeze blood from a stone."

The mayor's representative said, "So you admit you have never paid taxes?"

He said it like he was convicting Kapono of something, but before Kapono could answer, the big haole man with the fat gut had picked up one of the *'ili'ili nemonemo*, one of the little male stones, and turned it round and round in his big hairy hand. Kapono didn't really like to see the way the fat short fingers fondled the little stone.

"These would be great garden stones," the man said, as he cast his eyes covetously over the long expanse of

177

little stones that stretched across the beach as far as a man could see. "A guy could make a fortune selling these to landscapers in some of the big landscaping businesses in Kona and Waimea."

"Or you could ship them to the mainland," another man said. "Everything Hawaiian is big on the mainland these days."

The big haole had turned the stone around and around and then, before Kapono in his surprise could stop him, he spat on the pebble and began wiping it with his hand until it shone. Kapono clenched his fingers and was about to snatch the little stone from the man's grasp, when, holding it like a little saucer, the man threw it high up in the air, high up until it disappeared into the sunshine, and all the men had paused and listened silently as it came down invisibly with the sound of a clink.

Kapono, who could be quick to anger when the occasion called for it, for indeed he had once killed a man in quick anger, nevertheless was a man of patience when dealing with the ignorant. He had learned this patience over the many years the tourists and surfers had come down here to his beach, and even with the *'a'e kapu*, the trespassers with bad intentions, he had practiced patience, and had not broken their necks. The locals, of course, he never had a problem with, though as a matter of fact, they didn't come down here much. They liked better now to sit in front of a TV with a six-pack and grow fat, in Kapono's opinion.

The surfers usually had a *pono* attitude, a right attitude, and he often invited them to stay in the evening and share a little fish wrapped in fresh *limu* with him, which he cooked in the open pit. In this way, he taught them about sharing. In fact, he often looked on them as if he were a guardian, and had on occasion pulled a few of them out of rough waters, for though he was a small man, he was a strong swimmer, and knew the sea well. When

178

the surfers came now, they were always quiet, walking in single file barefoot on the stones, with their eyes on the sea, knowing their purpose—to lose themselves in the magic of the surf. They called Kapono "Uncle."

He had taught them and they had listened and followed his teaching. When they came down from the road carrying their surfboards, they would stop at the top of the trail and stand reverently, silently asking permission to enter the sacred 'aina. He had taught them that.

"You gotta ask permission," he said. "You gotta tell the gods and spirits who you are, and what you want, what for you are on the 'aina. And above all you gotta give *mahalo*. You gotta say 'Thank you.' That's the most important of all. That's the most important word in the Hawaiian language. Mahalo. *Mahalo nui loa. Thank you very much*."

He had taught them about the many spirits abiding on the 'aina, and about the *mana*, the spiritual energy of the 'aina, and how it must be respected, and how they too became a part of the mana of the 'aina, just by being there.

"You see, you haoles," he would joke with them, "the 'aina is like those big cathedrals you build, only bigger. You enter with respect. You be quiet. You act your best. You think pono thoughts. You no think bottom feeder thoughts. You don't take nothin' on the 'aina. You don't leave no trash. You no throw trash on the altar."

"You see," he would say, "the biggest cathedral in this world, the real church, is the sky, the sea, the soil. I am not the only kahu here; we are all kahus. And for this, we are humble. We humble ourself and ask forgiveness when we make mistakes, when we forget we are kahus."

A shiver of happiness and gratitude would run up his spine every time he said this, and he had said it many times over the years.

179

"*E malama pono i ka 'aina, nana mai ke ola*," he taught them. "Take good care of the land; it grants you life."

Yes, the surfers learned well, and they always brought him a beer, or a bud, or maybe a pizza—a present for him, the kahu of the 'aina. And he always accepted their gifts humbly, just as in the old days the kahu of the 'aina received the pig or banana or coconuts.

They would smoke the bud sitting around the fire and Kapono would talk story.

"See those stars," he would say, pointing up to heavens. "Know how come they got there?"

The surfers would shake their heads, and Kapono would tell how things came to be.

"In the beginning everything was nothing. Just black. Nothin' at all. Like the darkness of night. Along came Kane, the God of Creation. And then things start happening. There was a swirling in the dark. Kane, he picked up one giant gourd, and threw it into the sky where it broke into two pieces. The top half, curved, became the sky, and the seeds in the gourd spewed out and became the stars. The other half fell down, down and became the Earth.

"Then Kane filled the Earth with all the living things —birds, caterpillars, butterflies, dragons, turtles. Also he filled the Earth with great trees—the *koa*, the *kukui*, the *wiliwilli*, the 'ulu. And on the ground he spread *'uala*, the sweet potato, and *kalo*, taro.

"And then Kane took a mound of rich red earth, moist and sweet smelling, and made the shape of a man, and he breathed the sweet breath of life into him, and he came to life. And this was the first man, kane. And then Kane created for the man a wahine, and he breathed sweet breath into her too. And she came to life. And she was *nani koki*. I mean the most beautiful wahine like you never saw

180

before. She was babelicious! And he placed them both in *Paliuli*, paradise, a tabooed sacred land."

Here Kapono would pause. Sitting back on his elbows he would look up at the stars and think about that *wahine* for whom he had killed a man, and then he would think about a certain pretty hippy chick, and then he would think about wahines in general, about their silky hair and the velvety hairs on their arms. Then he would sigh and go on.

"And in Paliuli there was this beautiful crystal lake, deep without one bottom, all shining and bright, bright as moonlight. All silvery and bright. Like one full moon was deep in the lake. And this lake fed three crystal rivers. Waters of life. Bright and silvery as moonlight."

Again Kapono would pause. Thinking of the crystal rivers, the waters of life, that which nourished a man, made him think again of a *wahine 'ili a'ia'i*, a woman with skin fair and clear. For wasn't a woman with her silky hair and smooth skin the same as the waters of life? Didn't both nourish a man?

"And the three crystal rivers ran through Paliuli, watering all the 'ulu and *'ohi'a'ai* trees, the breadfruit tree and the mountain apple tree, which were *kapu* trees, special sacred trees and not to be messed with. So all good things were given to the kane and his wahine, and all good things grew there without no work."

"Sounds good to me, Uncle," said one surfer.

"And you know what they did there?" Kapono would ask, and he would look serious, like when he asked the tourists how it was all the little stones, the 'ili'ili hanau, covered the beach as far as one could see.

"They would lay beneath a 'ohi'a'ai tree. They would make a little bed. In like a little nest of soft leaves and grass. Like two little *'o'o* birds. You know the sweet sound of the 'o'o bird?"

181

The surfers would look blank and Kapono would continue.

"No, you don't know the sweet sound of the 'o'o bird, cause the 'o'o bird is long *make*, dead. Nobody living has ever heard the 'o'o bird. But it was called the 'o'o because it made one sound like this—'*oh, oh.*'

"So the kane and his wahine would have this little nest under the sacred trees. And the 'ohi'a 'ai blossoms, bright pink, would fall all around them like *kili nahe*—like a light, soft, gentle rain there would be all these bright pink blossoms falling all around them. And above them would float the pink and gold *ao akua*, the cloud islands of the gods. And from the pink and gold cloud islands of the gods would come walking Lilinoe, the Goddess of Cool Mists, walking down from the cloud islands on the path of a rainbow, floating down like on the wing of a bird, dressed in the finest golden *kapa* made from the rays of the sun, and she would spread a silver veil all around the kane and his wahine, so that all the land, the three crystal rivers, looked like one dream of beauty, so that the kane and wahine, wherever they looked, they saw beauty—if they looked into one another's eyes, they saw beauty, and if they looked out across the land with the three crystal rivers —everything that they saw was beautiful. And the kane and his wahine, *ua uhi 'ia ko laua mau mana'o i ke aloha.* Their thoughts were overwhelmed with love.

"So the kane and his wahine, in their soft nest, they made sounds like the 'o'o bird—'*oh, oh,*' they would whisper to one another. The wahine would whisper '*oh, oh,*' and then the kane would answer '*oh, oh.*' Like lovebirds, you know."

Here the surfers would smile.

"And they just made love, for hours and hours, never ending, singing sweetly like the 'o'o bird."

"Sounds good to me," one of the surfers would likely say.

182

"Sounds like paradise," one surfer might say. "What happened, Uncle?"

"The thing about Paliuli is you had to be a good man to stay there, a righteous man. You had to obey the god Kane. If he tell you do something, you had to do it. Some say some kind of *pilikia*, some trouble happened," said Kapono. "Some say the kane and wahine had to leave because they disobeyed Kane; they did something not pono. Some say it had to do with the two sacred trees."

"Paradise lost," said a surfer.

"Nothing good lasts forever," said another, and he sighed.

Kapono took a long drag of smoke and glanced up at the stars. Then he said softly, "You know what I think though? I think those people who say that are total wrong. I think kane and wahine are still there. I think they are still making love all day and all night. I think they are still making little sounds like the 'o'o bird. I think the wahine is still whispering '*oh, oh*,' and the kane is answering back, '*oh oh*.' I think Lilinoe the Goddess of Mists is still walking down a rainbow path spreading a silver veil all over the land, so that every time kane and wahine look up, they see a vision like no where else—a land all beautiful, with the sacred crystal rivers. A land like magic. It's all still there."

And Kapono and the surfers would go silent, thinking about Paliuli, paradise.

Yes, the surfers were all right. They had respect.

With the *'a'e kapu*, the trespassers, on the other hand, those who tried to steal the stones, or dig up the bones, Kapono's patience took another form.

There were those who came in broad daylight with big plastic garbage bags and just starting filling them up with the little stones like they owned them.

He would run up to them, waving his hands wildly.

"What are you doing?" he would yell.

183

They would inevitably act surprised, quickly dump the stones they had collected in a pile, and, apologizing, say they thought the beach was a public beach and that they thought they had the right to collect his stones.

"Would you go into a man's house and take out his furniture?" he would ask, trying to shame them.

That is how his patience took another form. He refrained from punching out their lights.

"Sorry," they would say. "We didn't realize."

But then there were those who came stealthily in the night, by moonlight or flashlight, who knew what they were doing was not pono, who clearly knew they were doing wrong. They would talk in whispers as together they would heave one of the heavy pillars and begin struggling back toward their truck hidden on the far side of the road above. Kapono though, attuned to the screams of the pebbles in the surf, would always hear them. Coming upon them in the shadows of the clouds, he would roar like thunder, like *ka'a ka pohaku*, like the stones roll, and they would drop their load and run as fast as they could, which was not too fast, over the stones. Kapono would pump his fist up in the air angrily and yell, "*Piko pau 'iole!* And don't ever come back down here!"

That is how his patience took another form; he didn't buss'm up!

In the old days, in the times of his father and his father's father and his father before that, no one would have dared to take even one small stone. Indeed, no one would have ever even thought of it. In those days, the kahu o ka 'aina, the keeper of the land, did not have to get up in the middle of the night and stop people from stealing the very land.

Then there were those who were truly ignorant but forgivable, the suntanned, almost naked hippy kids. They would bring *ti* leaves, gotten from who knows whose land, and take stones and wrap them up, and leave them for

184

"offerings" at the base of the stone pillars. Kapono had no idea who they thought they were offering to, and on occasions when he had wandered over and asked, the half naked hippies would look up at the sky and intone dramatically, "the gods." They would hold hands and drape themselves over one another and make a circle and sing in loud voices to earth mother or moon goddess, and the pungent smell of *pakalolo* would waft above their heads. He didn't have the heart to tell them to pipe down or tell them that their offerings would tomorrow be dismantled, and besides, he didn't really mind the half-naked pretty hippy chicks who smiled so bedazzling at him.

Once, one sun-drenched blond-haired blue-eyed chick, clearly stoned out of her mind, had even walked over, kneeled, and gracefully laid a big red flower on his foot, and then had looked up at him and smiled with half-closed dreamy-looking eyes while she folded her hands like she was praying! He had never figured that one out, but then it had happened only once.

"Too bad," he had thought. He had had the slight expectation that the girl might come back alone some day and visit him. Even better, some night! But too bad, he had never seen her again.

He would like to have a woman again. It had been many years since he had caressed the long brown hair of a *wahine*. It had been a long time since he had stroked with one finger the velvet arms of a woman, his mind on love. But he had spent long, long years in a prison because of a wahine. He had had to leave his beach and his father, and when he had finally returned, his father had died, and his brothers and sisters were scattered. Yes, he had killed a man for the love of a woman. Wrong doing like that stopped a man in his tracks.

He had heard, *he kehau ho'oma'ema'e ke aloha*. Love is like a cleansing dew.

185

But not for him. He could never forget that he had killed a man.

His father, his father's father, and his father's fathers before that, stretching back way into the past, had been the kahu here, had lived their lives in the arms of this 'aina. He had thought to do the same.

He had thought sometimes in earlier days, but who would come after him? If he had no woman, if he had no child, who would care for the 'aina?

He hadn't liked to think of it, so he hadn't.

The tourists were something else. They came talking loudly and laughing and boisterously, wearing neon colored sneakers and clunky sandals that crunched the little stones as they trod over them, so that he could hear them coming from a long way away. They carried plastic bottles of water that they often left behind, and after they had gone Kapono would find thrown in among the little stones silver foil candy wrappers gleaming in the sunshine.

"Wow!" the tourists would exclaim, loudly, as if they were all hard of hearing. "This place looks like Stonehenge or something!"

For among all the hundreds of thousands of small 'ili'ili hanau that covered the beach and the 'aina above the beach, as far as a man could see, were placed in some kind of order that not even Kapono could explain, even though he was the one who had placed them, the large stones, two or three feet or four feet high, standing upright like pillars of righteousness. They meant something, their cryptic arrangement meant something to the 'aina, to the sparkling sea, to the sun shining brightly in the midday, to the stars pouring starlight over them at night, to the bones that lay sleeping nearby, but what they meant, Kapono could not say in words. The upright stones were a message that was encoded in his breast, in his heart, as simple as a binary code, but as enigmatic as time without beginning.

He would approach the tourists and show them the proper way to show respect. *I mohala no ka lehua i ke ke`ekehi `ia e ka ua.* The *lehua* blossom unfolds when the rains tread on it. People respond better to gentle words than to scoldings.

"Aloha," he would begin. And then he would tell them about the birth pebbles of *Ko-loa*.

"They come from the mother land," he would say. "From many years ago. With the first people. They brought just two. And they put them here. And do you know why there are so many now?" he would ask, and he would look at them very seriously, and cock his head to one side.

"The male and the female come together. They create another, and the mother gives birth," he would say. "All things have a mother and a father."

The tourists would laugh, always. Then he would go on.

"This," he would say, and he would pick up the small smooth stone, and trace its smoothness tenderly with one finger, "is the male, the 'ili'ili nemonemo."

"And these," he would say, picking up a small pitted stone, "are the females. You can see that these pits are where the babies are held. When they are born, they drop from the mother. That is how all these stones you see here came to be."

He would hold the pitted stone in the flat of his palm, and stretch it out toward the tourists lovingly.

The tourists would giggle. Of course, sometimes they looked at him like he was crazy. Once in a while, the men reached into their shorts and pulled out a dollar, thinking that he wanted a tip.

Once though, a big pasty-looking man with a gut hanging out over his swim shorts had startled him by abruptly guffawing in an ugly way.

The man first took a long swig of his soda and then said in a nasty tone of voice, "You must be kidding. Do you tell everybody this crap? Why don't you tell the truth? Real science is a lot more interesting than some crapola superstitious nonsense."

The man took his soda bottle and swung it an arc, tossing out the remaining contents like a spray of vomit across the little stones.

Kapono had been so startled he couldn't even respond.

A pasty-looking boy who looked like a miniature of the pasty looking man, except that he was wearing bright green day-glow sneakers and purple tinted sunglasses with little rubber fishes on the sides, popped his gum, bent over and picked up one of the pitted pebbles, and looking up at the man said, "What's the real story, Dad?"

"The real story is the stones are created by molten lava covering them. Later, as the lava erodes away, the original pebbles fall out. That's all there is to it. Nothing magical about it. It's science. We're not in the dark ages."

The man grunted like a pig and laughed.

The boy grunted in imitation of the man, stuck his finger in one of the pits of the pebble, and held it up in the air. He twirled it around a few times until the pebble flew off his finger and sailed into the distance, landing with a bell-like clink. Then he spit his gum out on the stones.

This all happened before Kapono could react. For just a moment he was hurt, but then he was angry. For just a moment, it all seemed liked this had happened before, this huge anger that arose in him, that made him want to kill a man, but he didn't have time to think about that.

Not so much for the offense to himself, but for the offence to the little stones, for the offense to the 'aina, he said, "Get outta here," and he pointed toward the road up above. "Get offa my beach."

"*Your* beach?" said the man. "Are you saying you own this beach?"

"Yeah, I own this beach," said Kapono. "And my father before me and my father's fathers before him and back to all my fathers who first came here."

"It doesn't say that in this guide," said the man, holding up a gaudy-colored pamphlet with a girl in a grass skirt with coconut husks covering her boobs on the cover. "It says anyone can come down here. In fact, it says if you encounter a rascally old man who purports to own the beach, just ignore him."

It was only because of his surprise that Kapono had refrained from punching the guy.

"Well, anyone who respects the land, the 'aina can come here," said Kapono, "but if you don't have no respect, you can't come. So get outta here."

"You can't tell us what to do," the man had said. "We have every right to be here."

Kapono's face had so darkened and his eyes had become so lined with red blood veins and the muscles on his arms had so tensed that the man's pasty looking wife had visibly become really frightened, and touching her husband on the elbow, she said, "Let's go, honey."

"We have every right to be here," argued the man, but before he could say more, Kapono grabbed his arm and hurled him in the opposite direction. The man lost his footing and fell hard onto the stones.

"Get outta here now!" said Kapono

"We'll go," the man said, standing up and looking at a bleeding knee, "we'll go and call the police! You assaulted me!"

The man dropped the pamphlet down on the stones, and he and his wife and boy had clumsily fled as fast as they could back over the stones to their car.

"You need to learn some *aloha 'aina*," yelled Kapono.

From the safety of the car the little boy yelled back, "My dad could whip you good if he wanted to!"

It had taken a long time for Kapono's anger to subside after the tourists had left. He had stood and watched as they had driven away. Then he stooped and picked up the pamphlet with the girl wearing the coconuts on her boobs. He leafed through it until he came to a picture of his beach.

There was no mistaking it was his beach. There were the stone pillars, set among all the little stones, with the gleaming sea in the background. Even his little hut with the coconut frond roof was on the left side of the picture. The caption said: *Paradise Found!*

Kapono read aloud as he followed the words with his index finger. The article described his beach—"beautiful, unspoiled," "unique magical stone pillars," "sea turtles sleeping in the sand," "old temple with burial grounds"— and sure enough, it said: "If you encounter a rascally old local man who purports to own the beach, just ignore him. This is public property."

He was shocked. He was shocked on a lot of levels. He was shocked to see a picture of his beach, with even his house and the sacred stone pillars, in a cheap tourist publication with a girl wearing coconut husks on her breasts on the cover. It shocked him to think of how many people read this. He was shocked at the invasion of his privacy. And he was shocked to be called a "rascally old local man."

Rascally old man? He?

How many hundred, thousands, of times had he been kind to the surfers, advising them how best to get into the water, and even saving their lives when they disregarded his advice and went into the sea when it was too rough? How many times had he shared his fish with them in the evenings under the stars? How many times had he shared the story of the little stones with the tourists? How many times had he smiled graciously when their children had run amuck and pulled the stone pillars over, or peed right on the stones, and the parents had said nothing but smiled like it was so cute?

Rascally old man! He just couldn't believe it. He was neither a rascal nor old!

He read the article again, more slowly. But there was no denying it—they were talking about him. There was no other man who lived within miles of his beach.

He had walked to his fire pit and thrown the pamphlet down angrily. It would at least make good fire starter. Then he set off to fish. But the whole thing bothered him.

True to the pasty man's word, a few hours later two policeman came down the beach. Kapono knew them both, because they sometimes surfed here in their off hours, but they had never come down in uniform.

"Hey Uncle," one of them called to him. "What's this about you assaulting the tourists?"

The two policemen, local fellows like Kapono, looked at one another and laughed.

"I didn't assault nobody," said Kapono, and he told his story.

The police laughed and laughed, and Kapono even began thinking the whole thing was kinda funny, but nevertheless, the police had said, just before they turned to go, "Be careful now you don't get yourself arrested, Uncle. We gotta report this."

After they had gone, it occurred to Kapono that it was he who should have reported the tourists. He kicked himself that he had not thought to follow and get their license plate number. He should have reported them for trespassing. That would have fixed them good.

For several days the whole thing rankled his mind, his mind that normally was as peaceful and transparent as the sea on a calm day. He wasn't sure why it bothered him so much. After all, there had been other rude tourists. But on

191

the third morning when he was walking over to the *heiau*, the remains of which were as familiar to him as his right hand, he suddenly stopped and stared at a large sea turtle basking in the sun on the sand. Like a huge dark storm cloud suddenly blown in and casting a black shadow over the translucent sea of his mind, it occurred to him what was going to happen. He saw the portents as clearly as he saw *honu* there basking in the sun on the sand, calmly waiting to lay her eggs. His mind went to the many times he had had to wave the tourists away from the turtles, of how he had even found children sitting on the backs of the unresisting, helpless honus, screaming like they were riding a donkey. His mind went to the times he had found people digging around the heiau, where the bones of the ancestors lay buried, "looking for poi pounders," they said, "or bones."

Yes, he saw it all clearly. More and more of these tourists would begin to come, all because of the pamphlet with the girl wearing the coconut husks on her boobs.

He had to do something.

He was the keeper of the 'aina. It was his duty. He had to put a stop to it *now*.

He stopped being friendly to the tourists. He didn't greet them with aloha. He stopped telling the story of the little stones. He stopped telling the story of the magic turtle.

"They want a rascally old man," he thought to himself, "they get one."

Instead, he started yelling at them to "get offa my beach."

A man had a right to protect his home.

Now, with his chin still resting on his hand, still motionless, he thought back to the time when it first had dawned on him what the men with the measuring tapes and black note books meant. It had come as a sudden illumination, in the same way that long ago he had stood

192

over the still body of a man and realized with a small surprise—*He is make. Dead. I have killed a man.*

In the same way that he knew he had to act immediately when he saw the pamphlet with the girl with the coconut husks over her boobs, he went to work, and it wasn't easy. The next time the county officials came down, he confronted them outright.

"Get offa my beach," he said. "This land is not for sale."

Those four words opened the door to the fight. The country officials no longer traded knowing smiles with one another. Instead, they smirked, handed him a document and left.

Kapono had promptly ripped it to shreds.

All was quiet as usual for some weeks.

Then one morning Kapono was paid a visit by the highest official of the island, and his assistant.

The mayor offered his hand to Kapono, and they shook. The mayor then began to explain that he himself, in spite of his many duties, had come in peace to help Kapono understand that the land was going to be preserved for the future generations, that the burials needed to be protected, that the native plants and birds would be stewarded. In short, he hoped that Kapono would leave voluntarily.

Kapono was dumbfounded. Had not he and his father and his grandfather and his great-grandfather and his great-great-grandfather been the stewards of the land?

"If this is so, you must have documents to prove it," said the mayor.

"What kind documents?" asked Kapono.

"Legal documents," said the mayor, and he smiled craftily.

"My family was given this land by the King himself," replied Kapono. "The King's word is the word of a king. We don't need no documents."

The mayor and his assistant left, but being a gracious mayor, he gave Kapono ninety days to produce legal title to the beach.

"You gotta get a lawyer," the surfers advised Kapono, and one had given him a ride into town to visit a lawyer, but when the lawyer saw Kapono with his Hawaiian feet in his old cutoffs, he said, "My fee is $250 per hour. If you can't afford the fee, I can't afford the time."

"OK," said the surfers, "then you gotta get public opinion on your side. You gotta let the people know what is happening."

So they had written letters for him to the newspapers, while he himself had stood up on the road with a flag and a sign protesting the destruction of the ʻaina. At first the letters had generated a lot of interest and a lot of support from the locals.

Had not the islands been outright stolen? Had not the USA actually acknowledged the wrong done to the indigenous people, the *kanaka maoli*? Some wrote indignantly and angrily about the genocide of the islanders, while some pointed out that written deeds to the ʻaina were not part of a culture that had no writing. Some commended Kapono for his generations of stewardship of the ʻaina and the bones of the ancestors. They urged Kapono to "stand strong."

But in response the letters had gotten nasty, making ugly jabs against his character. When it came out that he had done time for murder, public opinion went against him. They started calling him a "squatter, just like a lot of other ghetto squatters on the beaches." They called him a fraud, and shiftless. They called him a tax evader, and accused him of running a place for the shiftless and homeless, of making the land dirty, of "staying on the land because he has nowhere else to go."

Some people wrote that he should be fined for trespassing, while another answered, "Why bother? You can't get blood out of a stone."

Squatter? He? And what about his father and his father's father and his father before that? Were they squatters? What did they mean about the "shiftless and homeless"? Were they talking about his friends? And why shouldn't he have "nowhere else to go"? This was his home!

And standing on the side of the road, waving the flag and pointing to the sign, had made him an object of ridicule. Some of the tourists slowed down to stare at him, and once in a while threw a dollar at him, but most people sped by without so much as a glance. Once a guy he recognized as someone he had once kicked off the beach for digging around the bones drove by, leered, and gave him the finger. And on one really bad day, he had returned to the beach to find that the Pohaku o Kane, the stone that sent dreams to the people on behalf of the god Kane, and offered them forgiveness when they had done wrong, and inspiration to make things *pono*, right, had been stolen. He saw the tire marks where a truck had driven right down, and the stone had been taken by thieves in broad daylight.

One night he had sat near the water's edge, when a couple of surfers came down. He couldn't offer them any *kaukau*, because he had not fished that day, having spent the entire day up at the top of the road, with his sign. They had brought him a pizza and a couple of beers. They hugged him and they were silent as he ate.

Then one of them cleared his throat.

"Uncle," he said, "we have heard that a big bio-fuel company is coming in, and they plan to level 20 square miles of the land around here, including the beach."

"What is bio-fuel?" asked Kapono.

"They're gonna make gas from algae."

"Not here. This is God's country," said Kapono. "This land has never been conquered."

"That was in the old day," said one surfer, "when a man fought hand to hand, eyeball to eyeball. These days you got to have money to fight. Lots of money."

"The bones of the ancestors will protect us," said Kapono. "The mana ..."

"The bones of the ancestors are going to end up in cardboard boxes in a Matson truck, like those they found when they built that Wal-Mart," one of the surfers thoughtlessly interrupted and said.

Kapono stared at him.

The surfers were silent.

One day soon after this news, the two policemen who sometimes surfed here came down to his hale with an eviction notice.

"You gotta go, Uncle," they said sadly.

They handed him the paper and walked away. The paper said Kapono had thirty days to remove himself and his belongings from the land.

Today was day thirty. The last day.

Kapono looked up at the blue sky. It was a brilliant morning, like it might have been the first day of creation. The sun shone like a gleaming gold coin, and the sea cliffs sparkled emerald green. The water was lapis lazuli deep blue, and diamond-capped waves raced the wind toward the beach. The little stones chattered and sang happily in the dancing turmoil of the breaking, foaming surf. Graceful and delicate *Manu-o-Ku*, White Fairy Terns, sailed overhead. The dozing honu lay buried in the warm sand, and the bones of the ancestors slept peacefully.

In all the days of standing up on the road with the flag and the sign, Kapono had never thought this day would really come. In all the talks with the surfers and with himself, he had never believed that one day all this would not be what he called home. Why, his mana was suffused with the mana of the 'aina. His mana was mixed with the mana of the honu and the bones of the ancestors and the sun and the clouds and the diamond capped waves and the green sea cliffs and the Manu-o-Ku. His mana was mixed with the mana of the little stones.

Be strong, his advocates had written to the papers. But not one of them had said, "*He hale kou*, you have a house, you are always welcome here—come Uncle, when you have no where else to go, come here."

Kapono looked toward the heiau where the bones lay resting. His father's father and his father before that, and his fathers before that were there. And now they would be dug up and put in cardboard boxes, like those bones in the Wal-Mart parking lot. Strangers who believed that stones were just stones and bones were just bones, wearing fingers in tight green plastic gloves, would handle them with indifference while they set their coffee mugs beside them and talked back and forth about what they did last Saturday night. They would make jokes and laugh while they nonchalantly scrubbed away dirt from the leg bones with old toothbrushes. They would talk idly about their plans for next Saturday night while they tagged the bones with numbers and glued skulls that were falling apart together again. Small bits and flakes of yellow bone would drop onto the floor, to be swept up later by a bored janitor and disposed into the trash.

Kapono felt first what was like a dull deep pain in the center of his chest, then something like a coiled wire snapping, then something like a knot in his heart quickly began to unravel, and then he heard like a great rushing of winds. A piercing, screaming sound filled Kapono's ears, and the earth shuddered violently, followed by a roar.

The ground opened, and the bones of the ancestors stood straight up in their graves; the 'ili'ili hanau, the little stones, were weeping red tears of hot blood! Bright red liquid seeped across the beach like a ghastly hemorrhage and flowed toward the sea. The honu struggled valiantly for a moment, but then her flippers became embedded in the sticky goo, and she became motionless.

A whirling chaos filled Kapono's chest. He looked at the sea but the waves were no longer rushing in; the diamonds on the water no longer sparkled but hung in the air like the tips of thousands of razor sharp knives. The sea was motionless and black as night and the sea cliffs above were like massive, cold, iron prison gates, open like jaws of death. The sun hung in the sky like an inkblot, and then began to melt. The white fairy terns were swallowed into the darkness.

Kapono's body jerked involuntarily. He didn't even have time to put his hand to his heart.

The whirling wind stopped, and all became dark and silent. Kapono lay on his back, his eyeballs glazed over.

Everything was black. Like the darkness of the darkest night. And quiet. Like the voice of a dead man. And still. For Kane, the God of Creation, had withdrawn the sweet breath of life.

And then above Kapono floated a pink and gold *ao akua*, the cloud island of the gods. And it floated gently, coming closer and closer to where the breathless body of Kapono lay.

And from the pink and gold cloud island came walking the Goddess of Cool Mists, walking down from the cloud island on the path of a rainbow, floating down as if on the gossamer wing of a bird, dressed in the finest golden kapa made from the rays of the sun. And as she walked she spread a silver veil all around, so that everything was covered with a soft, gentle, silver mist, like a dream of beauty. And the three crystal rivers flowed from the crystal lake, the lake all shining and bright like a full moon, and everywhere were the sacred trees, dripping with golden and pink and silver fruits. And the Goddess of the Mists spread a fine silver mantle over and around

198

Kapono and the woman who lay entwined in his arms, their thoughts overwhelmed with love.

Ua uhi ʻia ko laua mau manaʻo i ke aloha.

Their thoughts overwhelmed with love.

And sacred ʻohiʻa ʻai blossoms, bright pink, were falling all around them, like light, soft, gentle rain, like *kili nahe.* Soft, gentle rain. *Kili nahe.* And out of the silver mist, from under the fine silver mantle so gentle and soft that enveloped the man and the woman, came an enthralling song, rare and heard only by those who believe in magic, so that if anyone had heard it, they might have thought it sounded like the long unseen, the vanquished, ʻoʻo bird.

***

Ho'ola'i na manu i ke aheahe.

"The birds poise quietly in the gentle breeze."

Be at peace in the world.

****

Other works by Uldra Johnson (P. G. Johnson):

The Cry Room

Oklahoma Dust:
The Place Where a Story Ended
(P. G. Johnson)

Spiritual Not Religious:
Milking the ATM and Other Potent Stories

How the Universe Made Love to Petal Andersohn

The Wishfulfilling Jewel
(Book II of the Petal Andersohn series)

The Insider's Guide to the Best Beaches
of the Big Island Hawaii

The Insider's Guide to Hawaii Volcanoes
National Park, Including Volcano Village

Chalice of Love

****

Uldra Johnson is a multi-media artist. You can view some
of her other work at *VolcanoVillageHawaii.com*
or just google her name.

Made in the USA
Monee, IL
27 August 2022